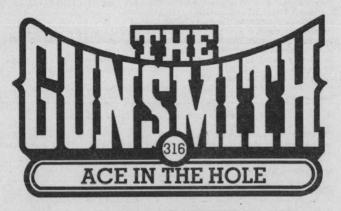

THE GUNSMITH

316

ACE IN THE HOLE

J. R. ROBERTS

JOVE BOOKS, NEW YORK

THE BERKLEY PUBLISHING GROUP
Published by the Penguin Group
Penguin Group (USA) Inc.
375 Hudson Street, New York, New York 10014, USA
Penguin Group (Canada), 90 Eglinton Avenue East, Suite 700, Toronto, Ontario M4P 2Y3, Canada
(a division of Pearson Penguin Canada Inc.)
Penguin Books Ltd., 80 Strand, London WC2R 0RL, England
Penguin Group Ireland, 25 St. Stephen's Green, Dublin 2, Ireland (a division of Penguin Books Ltd.)
Penguin Group (Australia), 250 Camberwell Road, Camberwell, Victoria 3124, Australia
(a division of Pearson Australia Group Pty. Ltd.)
Penguin Books India Pvt. Ltd., 11 Community Centre, Panchsheel Park, New Delhi—110 017, India
Penguin Group (NZ), 67 Apollo Drive, Rosedale, North Shore 0632, New Zealand
(a division of Pearson New Zealand Ltd.)
Penguin Books (South Africa) (Pty.) Ltd., 24 Sturdee Avenue, Rosebank, Johannesburg 2196,
South Africa

Penguin Books Ltd., Registered Offices: 80 Strand, London WC2R 0RL, England

This is a work of fiction. Names, characters, places, and incidents either are the product of the author's imagination or are used fictitiously, and any resemblance to actual persons, living or dead, business establishments, events, or locales is entirely coincidental.

ACE IN THE HOLE

A Jove Book / published by arrangement with the author

PRINTING HISTORY
Jove edition / April 2008

Copyright © 2008 by Robert J. Randisi.
Cover illustration by Sergio Giovine.

ISBN: 978-0-515-14449-9

JOVE®
Jove Books are published by The Berkley Publishing Group,
a division of Penguin Group (USA) Inc.,
375 Hudson Street, New York, New York 10014.
JOVE is a registered trademark of Penguin Group (USA) Inc.
The "J" design is a trademark belonging to Penguin Group (USA) Inc.

PRINTED IN THE UNITED STATES OF AMERICA

10 9 8 7 6 5 4 3 2 1

ONE

Clint Adams picked up the three cards he'd drawn from the dealer, added them to the two in his hand and slowly unfolded the five cards like a fan. He'd drawn another ace to go with the other two he'd been dealt. He folded the cards again so that they were stacked in his hands and waited for the other players to look at their cards and decide on their plays. He already knew this was the hand he was going to push.

The play was to Arliss Morgan, the local banker. When Clint had first ridden into the town of Virginia City, Nevada, he had had hopes of finding an interesting poker game, but he had never expected to be involved in a game with the town fathers. Across from him, in a floral vest with a very expensive watch fob hanging from it, was the mayor, William Tisdale. The other two men were local ranchers, Eric Greene and Joe Blocker. Eric was a big man people in town called "Hoss." He dressed more like a ranch hand than a ranch owner. Joe Blocker, on the other hand, was diminutive and a fine dresser.

The men had money, though, and were all secretly thrilled to be playing in a game with the famous Gunsmith.

They had been playing for several hours now, in a large

room on the second floor of the largest hotel in town, also owned by the banker, Morgan. The actual host of the game, however, was a fellow named Dave Hopeville, who owned the Red Garter Saloon and Gaming House. He was supplying the table, the cards, the chips, the refreshments and the girls who served the refreshments. A makeshift bar was set up in one corner of the room, and at the bar stood one pretty blonde and one striking redhead, in matching gowns of red and green.

Hopeville had owned many saloons and gambling halls all over the country, but he was a host, not a gambler. Clint knew him slightly from other towns, but did not know the man's past. It may have been that he'd never gambled, or at one time he'd gambled very badly and quit.

In Clint's experience bad gamblers never quit, they just kept going broke. He suspected Hopeville saw a way early in life to make money from gamblers without actually gambling against them. That made him a very smart man.

Hopeville was standing off to one side, holding a large cigar in one hand and mopping his shiny baldpate with a white handkerchief in the other. He wasn't nervous; he just had a habit of sweating a lot.

The banker, Arliss Morgan, rested his hands on his protruding belly and regarded his cards with a frown. Clint had already noticed that this was the countenance the man took on when he was about to bluff.

"I bet five hundred," he said, tossing the chips into the pot.

"Call," Hoss Greene said.

"I fold," Mayor Tisdale said, throwing his cards down in disgust. "I've got to stop trying to fill those straights."

The other men laughed and Joe Blocker said, "I'll take a look," and tossed in his five hundred.

"Raise a thousand," Clint said.

Morgan looked at him, narrowing his eyes.

"Are you bluffing, Mr. Adams?" he asked.

"No, Mr. Morgan," Clint said, "you are."

Morgan looked stunned and considered his cards for a moment before folding with a "Humph."

Hoss Greene laughed and said, "He got you that time, Arliss." Then he looked at his cards, dropped them on the table and said, "Got me, too."

Joe Blocker looked at Clint, then at his cards, and said, "I gotta keep lookin', Mr. Adams. I call." He dropped a thousand dollars' worth of chips into the pot, which was the largest of the day, almost ten thousand.

"Three aces," Clint said, fanning his cards on the table.

"I almost raised you," Blocker said, showing his three kings. "But in the end, I believed you."

"But you still had to pay to look, right?" Hoss asked.

"Oh, yeah," Blocker said with a smile. "I had to see those cards."

Clint raked in his chips and began to stack them.

"Break for refreshments, gents?" Dave Hopeville asked.

"You got some cold beer back there, Dave?" Arliss Morgan asked.

"Just brought in a cold keg, Arliss."

"Sounds good to me," the banker said, standing up.

"Me, too," Clint said. He rarely, if ever, drank while he was playing cards—at the table.

All five men stood and stretched and made their way to the bar, manned by the two pretty saloon girls.

Clint finished stacking his chips and walked over to the bar, where the striking redhead handed him a beer and gave him a smile.

"You're winning all the money," she said.

"Not all of it," he said, "but enough."

"Are you going to play all night?" she asked.

"I don't know, Loretta," he said. "I guess that depends on how long it takes me to go ahead and win all the money."

"I can wait in your room," she said in a low voice.

"That would be great," he said. She certainly knew where

his room was. She'd spent all night in it, and in the bed, with him.

She moved off to help the blonde, Andrea, serve the other men. Andrea had been in his bed the night before. It had made him nervous when he'd walked into the room and seen the two girls setting up the bar, but they had either not compared notes, or they had and didn't care. The possibilities inherent in the second case were endless.

As he drank his beer, the banker, Arliss Morgan, came up next to him, holding a cold one.

"I usually prefer brandy," the man said, "but sometimes there's nothing like a cold beer."

"Agreed."

"You're playing very well."

"Thanks. You're . . . holding your own."

"No," Morgan said, "I'm not, but it's nice of you to say. I wonder . . ."

"Yes?"

"After the game—whenever it ends—would you be open to talking with me?"

"About what?"

The banker shrugged and said, "Possibilities."

"I'm always open to possibilities," Clint said.

"Excellent," the man said. "We'll talk later."

The man drifted over to his neighbors and Clint wondered what that was all about.

TWO

The game didn't go all night, but it did go deep into the night, so that when they were done, the banker said to Clint, "Come and see me tomorrow morning."

"Sure, Mr. Morgan," Clint said. "Right after breakfast."

"Why don't we have breakfast?" the man asked. "Meet me in the dining room of the Stockman Hotel. Eight a.m."

"It's kind of late, Mr. Morgan," Clint said. "What do you say to . . . nine?"

"That's fine," Morgan said, "and please, just call me Arliss."

"Okay, Arliss."

As all the men were leaving, Hopeville came up to Clint and asked, "What's that about?"

"I don't know," Clint said. "I'm going to find out at breakfast."

"Well, make sure he pays," Hopeville said. "If it's not gambling, the man's a great skinflint."

"I'll remember that."

Clint looked around. Two other girls had come in to handle the bar a few hours ago and both Andrea and Loretta had been relieved.

"I've got to help the girls break down the bar," Dave Hopeville said. "How'd you do?"

"I did well," Clint told him. "I did very well. Thanks for getting me into the game."

"Well, one of the regulars canceled and I knew these men would get a thrill out of playing with you."

"I hope they were thrilled to give me their money."

"That's probably open to debate," Hopeville said. "See you tomorrow."

"I'll be around."

Clint left the room and went up one more level to the third floor, where his hotel room was.

Arliss Morgan entered his big house just outside of town. It was easily the largest house in town, two stories with antebellum white columns and a Mexican-style roof. He had designed the house himself and the mixture of styles was rather jarring, but he liked it.

"Is that you, Arliss?" his wife called from upstairs.

"Who else would it be?"

"Don't be cross with me, dear," she said, appearing at the head of the stairs. As she came down, he marveled again at the luck that had brought him a wife thirty years his junior. He knew they talked about them in town. How she was a gold digger and he was an old fool, but he didn't care. She was beautiful, and he'd do anything to keep her.

And she knew it. She made him jump through hoops, sometimes cruelly, but he still didn't care. It made him angry sometimes, but he still did it.

Now she came down and kissed his cheek. She was wearing a long, low-cut nightgown, and her generous breasts threatened to spill out. An ex–saloon girl and entertainer, at thirty-five she was still stunning.

"How did the game go? Did you win?"

"No," he said, taking off his jacket, "I lost. Big."

"You need a nightcap, then."

She went to a small sidebar they kept in the living room and poured him a brandy.

"I think I may have found our man, though," he said as she handed him the glass.

Her hand gripped his arm.

"Truly?"

He nodded.

"Who?"

"His name is Clint Adams."

"The Gunsmith?" she said with a sudden intake of breath.

"Yes."

"Will he do it?"

"I don't know," he said. "We're having breakfast in the morning to discuss it."

"Then you better come to bed and get some rest," she said, taking the brandy from him before he could finish it. "You have a big day ahead of you."

"With any luck," he said, following her upstairs. "With any luck."

THREE

Clint woke the next morning to the pleasant sensations of a firm, smooth little bottom being pressed into his crotch. He opened his eyes and found Loretta spooned back against him, her naked buttocks rubbing up and down him, making him hard. He reached around to caress her breasts, then ran his hand down over her belly until his fingers were buried in the red pubic patch between her legs. He found her wet already, so he lifted her leg and slid his hard penis up into her. She moaned, gave up any pretense of being asleep and began to rock back and forth, sliding him in and out of her. He moved with her, found her tempo, and the room quickly filled with the sound of flesh slapping flesh as they both enjoyed a quick, hard wake-me-up.

The had fucked themselves to sleep the night before, so a quick one to wake up to was fine with both of them.

"My God," she said as he got up from the bed, "I don't know if I'll be able to walk today."

"Who says you have to?" he asked. "Stay here and sleep some more."

"Oh, no," she said, stretching her long, lean body. "You woke me up good. What are you doing this morning?"

"I've got breakfast with the banker." He poured water from a pitcher into a basin and began to wash.

"Are you opening an account?" she asked eagerly. If that were the case, wouldn't that mean he was going to stay awhile?

"No," he said. "He's got something he wants to talk to me about."

"What is it?"

"I don't know." He dried his face, hands and chest, then wiped his armpits with the damp towel. "That's what he's supposed to tell me at breakfast."

"Well, be careful of him," she warned.

"Why?" he asked, getting dressed.

"There's talk around town that he may not be completely on the up-and-up. People are talking about moving their money to the other bank."

"The small one?"

"It's gettin' bigger," she said.

He strapped on his gun.

"Are you telling me he's crooked?"

She rolled onto her side and leaned on her elbow, staring up at him.

"He's got a young wife and people are sayin' that she's pullin' the strings. Everythin' was fine, they say, until he married her and brought her here."

"And when was that?"

"About three years ago," she said. "He went on a trip to San Francisco and came back with a young wife."

"How young?"

"About thirty years younger than him."

"Makes her . . . what? Mid-thirties?"

"I guess," Loretta said. "She's supposed to have been a showgirl in San Francisco."

"So she landed herself a wealthy older husband, huh?" he asked. "Isn't that every girl's dream?"

She reached her arms out to him and said, "You're every girl's dream, Mr. Adams."

"That's a nice thing to say," he replied, "but I'm not coming near you, because I'll just end up crawling into bed with you again."

"Would that be so bad?"

"It wouldn't be bad," he said, "but I've got things to do . . . and I'm hungry."

She slid her hands down her body until they were nestled between her thighs.

"I bet I could convince you."

"Maybe you could," he said, "but I don't think so. There are no strings on me, Loretta."

"And you know what?" she asked as he headed for the door. "That just makes you even better."

Clint made his way from his own hotel to the larger, more expensive Stockman Hotel. One of the reasons it was more expensive was because of the fine restaurant it had in addition to its comfortable rooms. Clint had chosen to stay in the second best hotel in town, the Carlyle House, because a friend of his had recommended it. According to his friend, the Stockman was overrated and overpriced.

But the restaurant was very good. He knew that because he'd already had a couple of meals there, breakfast and dinner.

When he walked in, he didn't see banker Morgan anywhere, and it looked to him like all the tables had been taken.

"Can I help you, Mr. Adams?" the maître d' asked.

"I'm supposed to meet Mr. Morgan here for breakfast. I don't see him and you look crowded."

"That's no problem, sir," the man said. "We keep a table for Mr. Morgan in the back. If you'll follow me . . ."

Clint did so, and the man led him to a large table toward the back of the restaurant, which suited Clint just fine. He took the chair with his back to the wall, ordered coffee and settled in to wait.

FOUR

At thirty-five, Tom Kent had been the sheriff of Virginia City for three years. Prior to that he'd held various deputy sheriff jobs around the country. He liked his job, but in three years he'd come to realize the things a sheriff had to deal with that a deputy never did. Like the town council and the mayor. Now, as he was walking down the street on his way to breakfast, he saw the president of the town council, the banker Arliss Morgan, coming toward him.

"Good morning, Sheriff," Morgan said.

As usual, the suit he was wearing had cost him more than the sheriff's horse.

"Mr. Morgan," the sheriff said.

"Off to breakfast?"

"Yes, sir."

"I'm going to the Stockman myself."

"A little too rich for someone on a lawman's salary," Sheriff Kent said.

"Well . . ." Morgan said, and kept walking.

The old fool had brought a young wife back to town with him three years ago—almost the same month Kent had gotten his job—and now he was trying to keep her.

Kent didn't think there was much chance of that.

*   *   *

Clint was on his second cup of coffee when Arliss Morgan walked in and was shown to the table.

"I'm sorry I'm late," Morgan said, sitting down. "I'm glad Walter took care of you."

"Walter?" Clint asked, then realized the banker was referring to the man who had shown him to the table. "Oh, right, yeah, thanks."

"I'll send the waiter right over," Walter said.

"Thank you, Walter. Oh, and my guest's breakfast will be on my check."

"Very well, sir."

Clint picked up the coffeepot and asked, "Coffee?"

"Yes, thank you." As soon as Clint finished pouring, Morgan picked up his cup and sipped. "It's good, isn't it?"

Clint had had better, but he nodded and said, "It's fine."

"I don't mind telling you," Morgan said, "I was impressed to learn that you would be playing in our game, but that was because I knew your reputation."

Clint remained silent. He didn't know what the man was getting at, but he was willing to let him get there in his own time. After all, he was paying for breakfast.

The woman took the man's penis fully into her mouth and suckled it. He gasped and lifted his hips off the bed. She did things to him he'd never had a woman do before. She was bold, and aggressive, and he couldn't get enough of her.

She released him from her mouth, straddled him, reached beneath her to take him in her hand and guide him to her. Then she sat down on him, taking him inside slowly. She was hot and wet as she started to ride him up and down. He reached up for her full breasts, squeezed them in his hand, thumbed the nipples. She didn't seem to notice. She was completely entranced by what was happening between her legs. She began to bounce up and down on him, pressing her hands down on his chest, taking her weight on her legs.

She was more squatting on him, not sitting, and she was in total control. At one point she lifted herself up and off him and he reached for her to pull her back down on him.

"Beg," she said.

"What?"

"You want to keep fucking me, don't you?"

Her mouth. He'd never heard a woman talk like she did.

"Yes, yes, I do," he said.

"Then beg for it," she said. "Tell me how much you need me, or I'll leave."

His penis was swollen and red and prodding the air.

"Please," he said.

"Please what?"

"Please, let me . . . back in."

"To do what?"

"To . . . to fuck you."

"Honestly," Diane Morgan, wife of the mayor, said, "for a lawman you talk like a Quaker."

"Come on," he said, "fuck me."

"Ah, that's it," she said. She lowered herself so she could run her wet, swollen pussy lips on the head of his penis. "What's the magic word?"

He reached for her and said hoarsely, "Please."

"That's it," she said, and swooped down on him, engulfing him.

FIVE

"It's your poker playing that truly surprised me," Morgan said.

"You expected me to play badly?"

"Well . . . no," Morgan said. "I didn't mean any disrespect. No, Dave wouldn't have brought you into the game if you played badly. No, no, we're all good poker players. It just surprised me how . . . easily you took our money."

Clint considered the situation for a moment, then thought, Oh, what the hell.

"Can I be frank with you without insulting you?" he asked.

"Of course," Morgan said. "Feel free."

Clint took a deep breath, then said, "You're all terrible poker players."

"I beg your pardon?"

"That's why it was so easy for me to take your money," Clint said. "You each have a tell that gives away when you're bluffing. I picked them all up within the first half hour."

"A tell?" Morgan asked. "I have a tell?"

"You rest your hands on your belly and frown whenever you're going to bluff."

Morgan stared at Clint in astonishment. "I do that?"

"Yes."

"What about the others?"

"I'm not going to tell you what their tells are," Clint said, "since you're probably going to continue playing with them. I'll just explain that the tells are there and very noticeable. All you have to do is look for them."

"I'll keep that in mind," Morgan said. "I'll also have to, uh, do something about my own, uh, little . . . tell."

"I suggest keeping your hands on the table for a while, until you get used to keeping them off your, uh, belly."

"Yes, well," Morgan said, "this makes my proposal to you even more, er, necessary."

After holding the pot out to Morgan and receiving a shake of the head in return, Clint poured himself another cup of coffee and waited.

"Some friends of mine and I are having a private game," Morgan said. "A very private game."

"Friends?"

"Men of considerable . . . holdings."

"Rich men?"

"Exactly."

"And where is this game taking place?"

"I'll keep that information, uh, private, if you don't mind, until you actually accept the proposition."

"Okay," Clint said. "When is this game to take place?"

"In a week's time."

"Well," Clint said, "you have time to do something about your tell."

"There will be a lot of money on the table," Morgan said, "a lot of money, and this is a winner-take-all game."

"How many players?"

"Six."

"From around the country?"

"From around the world."

"Interesting."

"Yes, it will be very interesting."

"And where do I come in?"

At that moment the waiter came with their plates. They both leaned back to allow him to set them down. After he was gone, Morgan picked up his knife and fork and asked, "Would you like to eat and then continue, or talk while we eat?"

"Let's have a couple of bites, and then continue," Clint said. "I'd just like to take the edge off my hunger so I can concentrate."

"Very well."

They both cut into their meat and began to eat . . .

Diane rolled over and away from her lover, Sheriff Tom Kent.

"That was . . . nice," she said.

Kent rolled to the other side, swung his feet to the floor and hung his head.

"What's wrong?" she asked. "Didn't you like it?"

"Don't ever do that to me again," he said.

"Do what, darling?"

He turned his head and looked at her from over his right shoulder.

"Make me beg like that."

"Oh, darling," she said, "that's just a game. If you don't like it, we won't play it again."

"I don't like a lot of your games, Diane," he said.

She leaned over and ran her hand down his naked back.

"But you'll put up with them, won't you?" She purred. "Just to be with me?"

"Don't always be so sure of me."

She got on her knees behind him, pressed her full breasts to his back, reached around and took hold of his penis. In her experience, no man could resist when put in this position. She began to stroke his cock until it started to harden again.

"I won't do it to you again, darling, all right?" she asked.

"Hmm, yeah, yeah . . ." He was starting to breathe hard again. "Okay."

She kissed his neck and ran one hand over his chest while continuing to work his penis with the other. It was just so wonderful to be with a young man—and a man younger than she was—after being around her husband. She had studied the men in town very carefully before choosing the young sheriff as her lover—and potential partner.

"Has your husband given you a clue yet about the game?" he asked.

"No," she said, "I still don't know where it's going to be. But I will. You are going to help me, though, aren't you, Tommy? Hmm?"

"I'm still . . . thinking about . . . it . . ."

She released her hold on him and scraped her nipples across his back as she got off the bed and onto her knees in front of him. From that position, she took hold of his erection again.

"Let me help you decide," she said, and slid him into her hot, eager mouth . . .

SIX

"The game was supposed to be private," Morgan said as they ate, "but as is usually the case with men of this stature, the word had gotten out."

"Cancel the game."

"We can't," Morgan said. "Certain parties have already come here from abroad."

"Move it."

"Again, we can't," Morgan said. "Our host insisted on the location."

"Your host?"

"Someone had to step up and vouch for all parties concerned," Morgan said, "and provide the location for the game."

"So you're stuck with the time and the place?"

"Yes."

"And what do you want me to do?"

"Well, initially," Morgan said, "my idea was to have you accompany me there, as sort of a bodyguard, and then function as a security consultant. For which you would be well compensated, of course."

"Of course."

"I say initially, as the idea struck me as soon as Dave

Hopeville told me you were in town and were going to play with us."

"But your idea changed?"

"Yes," Morgan said. "During the game."

"And what's your idea now?" Clint asked.

"Well, you would still be well compensated," Morgan said, "and you would still accompany me to the game."

"What's different?"

Morgan pushed his plate aside—he had decimated the breakfast in record time—and leaned forward. "I want you to play in my place."

Tom Kent left the small hotel on shaky legs. An hour with Diane Morgan exhausted him and exhilarated him at the same time. And in spite of the fact that Diane swore that the clerk was well paid to look the other way, there was the element of danger.

But the danger had only just begun. Diane no longer wanted just sex from him anymore, she wanted him to rob this big game her husband was planning. She told him she'd find out the time and the place, and that the rest would be up to him. She said they'd split the money— minus whatever he had to pay others for assistance—or they could simply keep the entire amount and go away together.

At a young age Kent had wanted nothing more than to wear a badge. Now, after years as a deputy and a few years as a sheriff, the novelty was wearing a little thin. The salary was terrible, the treatment he received from the town council even worse. The mayor, Diane's husband, and others bent the law to suit them, and it was his job to back them up. They'd made that clear. His job depended on it.

So why should he not take Diane up on her offer? He'd end up rich, and he'd have her, and they'd be living in Mexico somewhere.

The prospect was hard to resist.

*   *   *

After Kent left the hotel room, Diane reclined on the bed, still naked, and stared at the ceiling. Kent was a bull in bed, though easily controlled. Two of her favorite attributes in a man. She knew he'd go along with her plan to rob Arliss Morgan's big game, but she had no intention of going away with him. The man had limited imagination if he thought Mexico was the place to go when you were rich. She had much larger aspirations, like Paris, France, or maybe Rome, Italy.

And she certainly had no intention of taking a small-town, small-minded sheriff with her, or even of sharing the money with him.

Her hand drifted down over her breasts and her belly and then down between her legs as she thought about all that money, and about getting away from both her husband and Tom Kent.

SEVEN

"You want me to what?"

"Play in my place," Morgan said. "You see, there have to be six men at the table. It doesn't matter who, as long as the original six are backing them. Do you see?"

"So you want to stake me in that game," Clint said. "What's the buy-in?"

Morgan looked around to be sure no one was within earshot, then leaned forward and said, "One hundred thousand dollars each."

"You have that much money to risk in poker?" Clint asked.

"The risk is commensurate with the prize," Morgan said. "Six hundred thousand dollars."

Clint was able to do the math himself, but he let that pass.

"What's my cut?" Clint asked. "I mean, if I do this."

Morgan studied Clint and he could see the banker's mind working. How cheap could he get Clint?

"Ten percent."

Not so cheap, Clint thought. Sixty thousand.

"Do you know who else is going to play?" he asked.

"I know the five men who are putting up the money,"

Morgan said. "I know that two of those men will definitely want to play themselves. So there will be three others I don't know about. Why?"

"This kind of game could attract some pretty good poker players," Clint said. "Bat Masterson, Luke Short, someone like that might show up."

"And are you acquainted with these men?"

"Yes," Clint said, "very well acquainted."

"And do you find the prospect of playing against them . . . daunting?"

"No," Clint said, "not daunting. I've played with them before. But they are professional gamblers. At best, I'm a talented amateur."

"A talented amateur who was able to pick out the tells of four other men in half an hour. I find that impressive."

Clint told himself this man was a bad poker player. It didn't much matter what he found impressive. Still, sixty thousand dollars was a lot of money.

"What happens if I don't win?"

"Do you need a guarantee?"

"Of some sort," Clint said.

"I will cover all travel expenses," Morgan said, "and if we don't win, I will pay you five thousand."

Five thousand for playing and losing was almost irresistible. Well, okay, it was damned irresistible. But he didn't want to seem too easy.

"Let me think it over," Clint said. "When do you need to know by?"

"The game is Friday. We will have to leave on Wednesday. That gives you four days to decide."

"And if I don't go?"

"I'll have to hire a bodyguard and play myself."

"You'll be carrying your stake with you?"

"Yes," Morgan said. "I can't bring a bank note of transfer with me. There is no bank where we'd be going."

"I see."

Morgan leaned back, looked at Clint and asked, "Do you have anything better to do?"

Tom Kent went and had breakfast at a small café. When he'd run into Morgan on the street and found out he was going to breakfast at the Stockman, he knew the man would be busy for a while. He gave up his breakfast in favor of an hour with Diane. Now he was hungry.

Over breakfast of ham and eggs he thought about Diane's offer. He didn't know exactly how much money was involved, but she assured him it was a lot. Money and Diane were hard to resist, especially for a man who was disenchanted with both his job and his life.

If he was going to do it, though, he was going to need help. Not a lot of help, but the right kind of help. And he thought he knew just the man for the job.

He threw down his money for the breakfast and hurried out to his office. He still hadn't made up his mind about going through with it—about becoming a lawbreaker rather than a peacekeeper—but there was no harm in doing a little research.

Diane left the small hotel, blowing the young desk clerk a kiss. That, plus the money she paid him, kept him silent about the room she kept there. In the end, though, it really didn't matter if Arliss knew about it or not. He wouldn't do anything.

She walked through town, exchanging greetings with other women on the street who she knew talked about her behind her back. The whore that the banker had brought back from the West Coast. She didn't care. They were all prudish, shriveled women who were unhappy in their own lives but would never admit it.

She not only admitted it, she was going to do something about it.

EIGHT

Clint left the Stockman Hotel, while Arliss Morgan decided to have an after-breakfast drink. He also said he had some business to conduct in a part of the hotel that was a "private club."

"I'll get back to you on this as quickly as I can," Clint said.

"I will be over at Dave's place playing poker each night this week," Morgan said. "You can find me there. I'm going to have to work on purging myself of this tell."

As Clint left, he was thinking: If the man purged himself of his belly, he'd have a better chance of losing that tell.

On his way back to his hotel he passed a woman who reeked of sex. It wasn't that she smelled like it. It just immediately came to mind when he saw her. She belonged naked in a bed, not walking down the street, and not doing whatever it was she was going to be doing the rest of the day. She had long, auburn hair, full, thrusting breasts, and men and women alike watched her as she walked by. She ignored them all, however, except for Clint. As she passed him she locked eyes with him boldly, and when he looked back to watch her walk away she was also looking back at him. Another time, another place, he might have gone after her . . .

* * *

As Diane looked back over her shoulder, she saw that the man was looking at her as well. Some other time, she would have grabbed him and dragged him to a hotel. He wasn't like the other men in town. He walked different, wore his gun different, and he looked at her different.

As they went their separate ways, she wondered: Who was he?

As Clint turned away from the woman, he almost walked right into Dave Hopeville.

"Dave," he said. "Sorry."

"What're you lookin' at?" Dave asked.

"That woman. See her? Walking away?"

"Oh," Dave said.

"What? You know who she is?"

"Even from the back."

"Who?"

"That's Diane Morgan."

"Morgan?"

Dave nodded.

"Banker Morgan's wife."

"She is thirty years younger than him."

"At least."

"I can see why the women on the street look at her the way they do."

"And you already know why the men are lookin' at her," Dave said.

"Must be tough for a man that age to keep a woman like that happy."

"Money helps," Dave said.

"But money isn't everything."

"Well, I don't envy Arliss Morgan bein' married to her."

"You're probably the only man in town who doesn't."

"Don't get me wrong," Dave said. "I'd like to get her out of that dress as much as the next man, but I wouldn't

want to be married to her and have the problem of keepin'
her happy."

"You might have a point there."

"Where are you off to?" the saloon owner asked. "Or
coming back from?"

"Back from breakfast with Morgan."

"Ah," Dave said. "Did he make you an offer?"

"You know about his game?"

"Most people in our business do."

"Well, I'm not in your business," Clint responded, "so it
was news to me."

"I figured he'd be interested in you as a bodyguard of
some kind. Am I right?"

"You're right," Clint said, not bothering to fill the man
in on the rest of the offer.

"Well, if he offered you a bundle, hold him up for more
and take the job," Dave said. "It's probably not his money
anyway."

"What do you mean?"

"There's some talk in town about him and his practices
at the bank," Dave said.

"Like maybe he's using bank money?" Clint asked.

"To fund his gambling," Dave added. "You played with
him. He's terrible at it."

"Yes, he is."

"In fact, I'm on my way to the bank now. I'll see you
later tonight?"

"I'll be in," Clint said.

He headed back to his hotel, wondering if the hundred
thousand that Morgan was putting up for the game belonged to the people of Virginia City.

NINE

Clint spent the day thinking over Morgan's offer. Sixty grand was hard to turn down, five grand not as hard but still difficult. But if the money was coming from the bank—and coming out of the pockets of the Virginia City residents—could he, in all good conscience, take it? Maybe what he needed to do was confront Morgan with people's suspicions. Let the man explain, if he could, or simply convince Clint that the money he was putting up for the game was his own.

Late in the afternoon he went to the Red Garter and got himself a beer at the bar. His breakfast had filled him to the point where he was only just now getting hungry again. He thought to start with a beer and then go off in search of supper.

The Garter was just beginning to pick up. The covers had been taken off the gaming tables and men were starting to file in to play. The girls had just come down, preparing to work the floor. Clint saw Andrea, who smiled and waved, but he did not see Loretta yet. Also, Arliss Morgan was not present.

The bartender recognized him. Clint had to grope for his name but came up with it by the time the man brought him his beer.

"Thanks, Travis."

"Heard you took some money off the town fathers last night," Travis said. "Good for you. I been a bartender for over thirty years. Love to see somebody take the town leaders."

"How long have you been working here?"

"About three years."

Clint studied the man. If he had been a bartender for thirty years, he must have started in his late teens, unless he just looked good for his age.

"Fifty," Travis said.

"What?"

"You're wonderin' how old I am," the man said. "I'm fifty. I look good for my age, not a day over forty-five."

"And you're a mind reader."

"Comes with the job."

He went off to draw beers for some new arrivals just as Andrea sidled up to Clint

"Hi, handsome."

"Andrea," he said. "You're looking as lovely as ever."

"Sure, sweet-talk me while you're sleepin' with my best friend," she said. "I thought we had a good time the other night."

"We did."

"But you like Loretta better than me?"

"Well, no, not better—uh, I mean—just diff—"

"Relax, cowboy," she said, slapping his arm. "I'm just kiddin'. We're friends, we share. In fact, we kinda thought tonight we'd share you."

"Uh, tonight? Share?"

"Yeah, you know . . . as in, you, her . . . and me? Whataya say? You brave enough?"

"I think I could manage to dredge up the courage," he said.

All he had to worry about was dredging up the stamina.

Each woman had almost worn him out on her own. Both of them together? Now, that was daunting.

"We'll see you later, then," she said, stroking him beneath the chin.

He watched her walk away and thought that if he were a praying man, he'd say a prayer for himself.

Sheriff Tom Kent sat behind his desk, papers strewn across it. Telegrams, wanted posters, correspondence with federal sources. His suspicions were correct. Tito Calhoun was out of prison.

Kent knew Calhoun from when they were both young men. Kent had come west from Massachusetts; Calhoun had come north from Mexico, where his mother and father still lived. They met in Arizona, both working hands on a small ranch, and talked about what their futures would be like. Calhoun eventually joined up with a gang who robbed banks and trains. Kent got a job as a young deputy in a small Kansas cow town.

Kent remembered Calhoun as a man who was deadly with a knife and a gun. He'd heard that Calhoun had gotten himself sent to Huntsville Prison several years ago, but he thought that he had received notice recently that Calhoun had been paroled. After going through all his paperwork, he discovered that he was right.

So if he decided to go through with this, he had four days to recruit Tito Calhoun, and leave it to Calhoun to recruit a few other men.

That meant he was going to have to make his decision quickly, and act just as quickly.

At that moment the door opened and Mayor Tisdale entered. He had some inane request of the sheriff, something demeaning, and by the time the conversation was over Kent had made his decision.

TEN

Clint was having a second beer when the sheriff walked in.
They had met on Clint's first day when he'd gone and introduced himself to the local law. He wasn't impressed by
the young man, and Kent had managed to stay away from
him the whole time he was in town. He watched as the
young sheriff's eyes swept the room, and when they fell on
him the man visibly reacted. He stiffened a bit, took a stut-
ter step forward, then turned and left the saloon. Clint
shook his head, turned his back to the door and returned to
his beer. Kent wasn't going to get very far as a lawman being afraid of men with reputations.

Tom Kent cursed himself. He'd been staying away from
Clint Adams ever since the man arrived in town. He knew
the Gunsmith's reputation, and he felt uncomfortable
around the man, but that didn't mean he had to run every
time he saw him.

That was it, he thought. That was the deciding factor in
whether or not he was going to take Diane's offer: the
chance to give up wearing a badge, and stop having to deal
with men like Clint Adams. He checked his watch. He still
had half an hour to make the telegraph office.

* * *

"I'll be at the saloon," Arliss Morgan told his wife.

"Arliss," she said, "have you made up your mind yet?"

"About what?"

"You know what," she said. "Are you going to ask Clint Adams to go to your big game with you?"

"I've already asked him," he replied.

"That's wonderful." She clapped her hands together as if she was delighted for him. "And what did he say?"

"He's thinking about it."

She came up close to him, so that her perfume filled his nostrils, and she pressed against him so he could feel the heat of her body.

"I'm sure you'll get him to accept," she said. "You're so clever that way."

"Oh, uh, yes, I'm sure he will," Morgan said. "I've offered him quite a lot of money."

"Which is okay," she said, "because you're going to win a lot of money, aren't you?"

"I certainly hope so." He cursed his body for not responding to her. In his head he wanted her, but his body . . . At his age it took some doing to get him aroused, and he knew that Diane was getting tired of expending the effort for not much in return. He put his arm around her and said, "We are going to get a lot of money."

"Yes," she said, kissing his cheek and sliding her hand down his pants to give him a little squeeze, "we are."

Arliss Morgan was delighted that, as he left the house, he had the beginnings of an erection. Perhaps tonight, when he returned . . .

Diane Morgan watched her husband from the front window until he was out of sight. All she needed from him was the time and the location of the game. She'd asked him several times. But the last time he had become very agitated. She decided to bide her time and wait for just the

right moment before asking again. She figured tonight
would be the night. Get him hard, get on her knees in front
of him, control him. Just as she'd made Tom Kent beg, she
would make Arliss Morgan come across with the information she needed.

Then all she'd need was for Kent to agree, and the
arrangements could be made.

Six hundred thousand dollars, there for the taking . . .

Kent watched as Arliss Morgan left his house. He had sent
off his telegram and hoped that a reply would be waiting
in the morning. He had a good idea where Tito Calhoun
would go when he got out of jail. He just hoped that his
old friend was still there. He also hoped that prison time
had not taken the edge off him. In fact, maybe being in
jail would make that edge even sharper. If he knew his
friend—and he thought he did—he'd be angry and anxious
to get back at the world for putting him in a box.

Kent made sure the coast was clear before crossing the
street and moving around to the back of the Morgan house.
During the day, Diane made sure the kitchen door was always unlocked. And she made sure her husband did not
hire any servants for her, so she could do what she wanted
in her own house when her husband was in town.

Kent opened the door and entered, closing it behind
him. He had started toward the doorway that led from the
kitchen to the dining room when suddenly Diane appeared
there . . . naked.

"How did you know?"

"Sweetie," she said, "I can always smell you when you
want me."

ELEVEN

Clint was still on that second beer, contemplating either a third or a move to one of the poker tables, when Arliss Morgan came through the batwings. He spotted Clint immediately and came over to the bar.

"You're not playing?" Morgan asked.

"After our conversation, these games just didn't seem to attract my interest."

The banker looked over at the tables, and the people playing at them, and said, "I don't blame you."

"What'll ya have, Mr. Morgan?" the bartender asked.

"A beer, Travis," Morgan said.

"Comin' up."

"We could get up a game upstairs," Morgan said. "There's a small room and—"

"I'd rather talk about your game, Mr. Morgan."

"Arliss, please," the banker said, accepting his beer from the bartender, "call me Arliss. I have the feeling we're going to be in business together."

"Only if you can answer a question for me," Clint said. "And convince me that you're telling the truth."

"This sounds ominous," Morgan said. "What do you say

we finish these beers and then I'll take you over to my club. We can talk where it's quiet."

"Suits me," Clint said.

When they entered the Stockman Hotel, Morgan led Clint down a hall and through a doorway. Inside, a man stood and nodded to him as they went by.

"If you were here alone," Morgan told Clint, "you would not have gotten in."

Clint didn't bother telling Morgan that he didn't like private clubs and would never try to get into one.

They were in a large, high-ceilinged sitting room filled with overstuffed chairs of emerald green and maroon, crystal light fixtures and tuxedoed waiters.

"Every member has his own chair," he explained, "and a guest chair. Here we go."

They sat down on two chairs, with a low table between them. A white-haired waiter immediately appeared, wearing not only a tuxedo but also white gloves.

"Brandy, Jackson."

"Yes, sir. And for your guest?"

Clint thought a moment, then said, "The same."

"As you wish." The waiter executed a small bow and then withdrew.

Clint looked around the room. There were only a few men on the other chairs.

"It usually gets busier in the evenings," Morgan explained. "That's when our members come here to get away from their wives."

"Is that why you come here?"

"I have a beautiful wife, Mr. Adams," Morgan said. "I have no reason to get away from her."

"My apologies," Clint said. "I meant no offense."

"None taken."

"And I mean no offense with my next question, either," Clint went on. "It's just that I've heard things."

"Oh, my," Morgan said. "The rumors."

"Yes, the rumors."

"So you want to know if the money I'm using to stake you in this game is my money, or does it belong to the depositors? Do I have it right?"

"Yes, you do."

"I assure you, Mr. Adams—Clint. The money you will be playing with in the game is mine and mine alone. I do not need to steal my depositors' money."

Clint opened his mouth to ask another question, but Morgan raised his hand and stopped him.

"Your next question is: Why did the rumors start? It happened when I brought my wife back with me from San Francisco. She's quite a bit younger than I am, and the rumors started that I needed a lot of money in order to keep her. Well, I have a lot of money, Clint—quite enough to keep her happy for a long time. Does any of what I've said allay your fears? If not, then I'm afraid we must part company. I could show you my own personal bank account, but how can I prove none of that money came from other depositors?"

"I suppose you can't," Clint said.

"So my word will have to be good enough."

The waiter came with two brandy snifters on a silver tray. He held the tray right between them so they could both take their drinks, and then he withdrew again.

"What say you, Clint?"

Clint raised his glass and said, "I say we have a partnership—a ten percent partnership."

"Excellent," Morgan said, and they touched glasses.

TWELVE

"The game will take place at the home of a man named John Deal. He's a wealthy rancher who moved here from England several years ago. Oddly enough, he discovered poker when he moved here, likes the excitement of a high-stakes game, although he lacks the nerve to play."

"I thought you said he was rich."

"He is," Morgan said. "It's got nothing to do with the risk of losing. He just can't stand up to the pressure of sitting at the table. He prefers to host big-money games and watch."

"And where does this man live?"

"If you don't mind, I'll keep that to myself for now," Morgan said, "but it's only a day's ride from here."

"Are you up to a day's ride?"

"I haven't been on a horse in some time, but I think I can handle it."

"Do you have a horse?"

"I'll get one from the livery."

"To buy or rent?"

"Rent, I think."

"How about letting me pick it out for you?"

"That suits me fine," Morgan said. "Just tell them that

you're renting for me. In fact, I'll give you some money and you can make the transaction outright."

"That's fine."

"Will you need some money up front?" Morgan asked.

"Just a couple of hundred," Clint said. "If it's a full day's ride, we'll need to camp overnight . . . both ways. We'll just need a few things."

"All right."

Clint was surprised when Morgan went right into his wallet and handed him two hundred dollars.

"How about filling me in on who the other parties are?" Clint asked.

Morgan hesitated, and Clint said, "Okay, fine, I'll find out when get there."

"There will be no one there who is wanted by the law," Morgan said. "I can tell you that."

"That wouldn't have an effect on my decision," Clint said. "As long as he can play cards."

"Good. This is excellent. How about another brandy to cement the deal?"

"Don't mind if I do." Clint didn't usually like brandy, but he had enjoyed the first glass.

Tom Kent was on his knees behind Diane Morgan, who was on all fours on the floor in her dining room. If Arliss Morgan had come home at that moment, Kent knew he'd have to kill the banker.

"Come in, come on," Diane was saying, urging him on, "harder, damn it . . ."

He gripped both of her hips and pulled, so that every time he drove himself into her glorious pussy her marvelous ass slapped into him. Kent had never been so . . . obsessed with a woman before, and he'd had his share. Diane Morgan was unlike any other woman he'd ever known, and it didn't bother him at all that she was several years older than he was—and that was only if she was telling the truth about her age.

"Uhh, uhh," she grunted, every time she slammed back into him with her butt.

He started to move faster and faster, his cock feeling as if it was about to burst. He'd do anything for this woman, anything at all, and that included killing her husband or anyone else who got in the way of their happiness.

Diane continued to implore Kent to fuck her, hoping that he'd finish soon. She knew she had him; he'd already told her that he was in, and that he had already contacted someone about helping. She didn't mind a romp in the afternoon with her young lover, but this one had not come at the most opportune time. If Arliss walked in on them, she knew that Kent would have to kill him, and that would pretty much ruin her own plan. What had started out as a lark had now become potentially dangerous, so she was trying her damndest to get Tom Kent to finish . . .

"Hurry," she said moments later. "Get dressed."

"Let me catch my breath."

"Come on, Tom," she said, throwing his clothes at him. "Catch your breath outside. Arliss could be home any minute."

"That didn't seem to bother you when you greeted me in the kitchen, naked."

"That was stupid," she said. "It won't happen again. And don't come here again."

"I had to tell you," he said, pulling on his pants.

"Fine, you told me," she said. "Now get your people together so that when I have the location and the time you can move."

He got that look on his face men got when they thought they were being scolded, so she grabbed his shirtfront, pulled him to her and kissed him. She felt him growing hard in his pants, and as his hands reached for her she pushed him away.

"Get out already," she said, "before we end up on the floor again. I have to get dressed."

"I love you, Diane," he said, strapping on his gun. "I would do anything for you."

"I know, darling," she said, "I know."

She pushed him to the back door, opened it and gave him a shove outside. Then she threw him a kiss and closed it in his face. She needed a bath and a change of clothes.

Kent made his way around the house, made sure no one was there to see him, then crossed the street. Once there, he stopped to catch his breath and straighten his clothes, and then he started walking back to his office, remembering the first time he and Diane had had sex, in one of the cells.

All of a sudden he felt completely happy with his life, and where it was going.

THIRTEEN

Arliss Morgan decided to hone his poker skills a bit by playing in one of the smaller saloon games. Clint decided to go back to his room to make plans for this new job. Playing small-stakes poker wasn't going to do him any good. He also took the opportunity to clean his weapons.

He had finished with his rifle when there was a knock on the door. His grabbed his pistol, which was hanging in its holster on the bedpost and newly cleaned. He held the gun behind his back and went to the door.

"Who is it?"

"Andrea," a voice said.

"And Loretta," another voice said.

He frowned, then smiled. He hadn't thought Andrea was really serious about what she'd said, but apparently both women were. He opened the door and found them both standing there with smiles, shawls covering their dresses, bare shoulders and cleavage.

"I'll bet you thought I was kidding," Andrea said.

"Actually, I did think that," he said, "but I'm glad you're not. Come in, ladies."

They entered and Clint walked to his holster and replaced the gun.

"Were you going to shoot us?" Loretta asked, removing her shawl.

"I would have shot anyone but you," he said.

"You're sweet," Andrea said, removing her shawl. "Do you have anything to drink?"

"I'm afraid I don't."

Andrea brought a bottle of whiskey out from behind her back. "I swiped it from behind the bar. They'll never miss it."

"Did you bring glasses?" he asked.

She shook her head.

"I thought we'd all get naked and pass the bottle around."

"That works for me," Loretta said, slipping out of her dress first.

"Here," Andrea said, handing the bottle to Clint, "you open it and start while I get undressed."

He accepted the bottle, opened it and took a drink while Andrea's dress dropped to the floor. Both women were now naked, and Clint blessed the God that made women in a variety of sizes and shapes.

Loretta was long and lean, pale-skinned, with small breasts and brownish nipples. The patch of hair between her legs was like fire.

Andrea was shorter than her friend, even paler, with wide hips and big, rounded breasts tipped with pink nipples. Her pubic hair was like gold.

"Your turn," Loretta said.

Clint handed Andrea the bottle. She took a sip and handed it off to Loretta while Clint removed his clothes. Since he'd been in bed with both women before, there were no surprises here, but they all still stared at each other with approval.

Loretta handed Clint the bottle. Andrea ran her hand over Loretta's hip and asked Clint, "Doesn't she have a beautiful body?"

"You both have beautiful bodies."

"I'm so fat," Andrea said. "I wish I was long and lean like Loretta." She ran her hand across her friend's flat belly.

"You're not fat," Clint said. "You're lovely."

As if to prove it to her, he handed Loretta the bottle, then took Andrea into his arms and kissed her. She squirmed against him, thrusting her tongue into his mouth. When they broke the kiss, he reached out and pulled Loretta close. When they kissed, she passed some whiskey from her mouth to his.

"Mmm," he said as some of it ran down his chin, "it's even better that way."

Andrea licked the whiskey from his chin and said, "Oh, you're right. And I bet I know another way it's good."

She looked at Loretta and the two women seemed to transmit a thought to each other. They pushed Clint to the bed and down onto it, then got on either side of him. Loretta poured some whiskey into his belly button, which Andrea slurped up. Then the blonde took the bottle and poured some of the liquor onto his penis, and the redhead licked it off. By the time she was done, he was fully erect.

"You missed some," Andrea said. She leaned over him and engulfed him in her hot mouth. At the same time Loretta bent and kissed him. Then she poured some of the whiskey onto his chest and began to lick it off. With both women's tongues and mouths working on him, he began to squirm.

Andrea released him from her mouth and said, "Come on, Loretta, honey, you're missing out."

Loretta got down between his legs and took him into her mouth, after passing the bottle to Andrea. It was nearly empty, so she finished it and tossed it away, then moved up to sit on Clint's chest so he could lick her. He slid his hands beneath her ass and started working on her vagina enthusiastically. She reached out to take hold of the bed rail and moved her hips, moaning as he licked her. Meanwhile, Loretta was fondling Clint's testicles and sucking him avidly. He couldn't see her, but suddenly she released him from her mouth, and then he felt her straddling him. She took hold of his penis, guided it to her vagina and then sat right down on him. The two women were now both riding him and he thought that if he had a heart attack and died right there, he'd die a happy—and lucky—man.

Later the two women woke him up by passing his rigid cock back and forth to each other. At one point they were both licking it, and he had one hand on each of their heads. Finally, he decided to turn the tables on them. He got to his knees and flipped each of them onto her back. First he buried his face in Loretta's crotch, at the same time sliding his fingers in and out of Andrea's pussy. He sucked on Loretta until she screamed and pushed him away, and then he switched to Andrea, who opened her legs wide for him, holding onto her ankles. He ran his tongue up and down her wet slit, every so often driving it into her like a small penis. Finally, he concentrated his actions on her core, sliding one finger in and out of her, and then two, until she was gushing all over his face. She grabbed his head and pushed him away as Loretta had done. He got to his knees and looked at both of them as they tried to regain their breath.

"Oh, God," Loretta said, "he's tryin' to kill us."

"Yeah," Andrea said, "but what a way to go."

"Just give us a few minutes, big boy," Loretta said, "and we'll take care of you."

"We have to get some sleep, girls," he said. "We need to call a truce until morning."

Andrea smiled and said, "Well then, snuggle on up here between us, you beautiful man."

"Okay, but no tricks," he said.

"No tricks," Loretta said, "honest. We promise. You tired us both out."

He slid between them and they pulled the sheet up over the three of them. Each of the women pressed herself against him, putting her head on his chest, and he encircled them both with his arms. Their hands strayed—he ran his middle finger along the cleft between their buttocks, while they rubbed his belly and brushed against his penis—but it was all halfhearted, and finally the three of them fell into a deep sleep . . .

FOURTEEN

Arliss Morgan came home and found his wife sitting in the living room with a glass of wine.

"There you are," she said, without getting up from the sofa. "I was about to send the sheriff to find you."

"I was at the saloon."

"Did you see Mr. Adams?"

"I did."

He walked over to the bar and poured himself a glass of wine, then joined her on the sofa.

"Is he going to do it?" she asked.

"He is."

"Oh, darling," she said, "that's wonderful." She held her glass up and he clinked it with his. "That's just what you wanted. I'm so happy for you."

"For us," he said. "This will mean a lot of money for us, Diane."

"I know, darling," she said, "but it's all due to your cleverness." She leaned over, laced her hand on his crotch and kissed his neck. She kneaded him through his pants until she felt a stirring.

"Uh-oh," she said into his ear, "I think someone needs to go upstairs."

"No," he said, "right here."

"Here? In the living room? How decadent you are, Arliss."

He didn't want to tell her that he was afraid that by the time they got upstairs his penis would be soft again. Her hand through his trousers had aroused him and he didn't want to take a chance on missing out.

Obediently, she got to her knees in front of him and undid his trousers. He lifted his hips so she could slide them off, then took his semi-hard penis into her hands. She stroked it, and cooed to it, but it refused to get fully hard until she finally took it into her mouth.

Arliss Morgan put his head back and let out a contented sigh . . .

Diane worked her husband's penis until he was ready to burst, then she took him from her mouth and began to stroke him with her hand.

"No," he said, "in your mouth—"

"I want to see it, darling," she lied. "I want to watch you . . . please . . ."

"Oh, all right," he said. He couldn't refuse her anything when she had him in this state.

The truth of the matter was she didn't want her husband ejaculating into her mouth. This was good enough for him. She could hear his breathing quickening and then he lifted his hips, groaned aloud, and his penis shot a small amount of semen, which simply trickled down his shaft. It was all he was good for these days, she thought, no matter how hard she tried.

"There you go," she said, hoping he wouldn't want her to lick it off. "Now how about some leftover roast? And then you can finally tell me all about your plan."

FIFTEEN

Clint killed time for the next two days. He sat on a chair in
front of his hotel during the day, went to the saloon in the
evenings, and spent his nights with either Andrea or Loretta
or both. It was amazing to him to be able to find two women
who were such good friends that they could share a man.

He also went to the livery and found a horse to rent for
the banker, although he was wondering if he shouldn't get
a buggy for the man instead. After all, Morgan was in his
sixties and had spent many years behind a desk. He decided to ask him about it the day before they were to leave.

He picked out what supplies they'd need and told the
clerk at the general store that they'd be picking them up at
the end of the week. The man said since it was for the
banker, Morgan, he'd open early Friday morning and have
it all ready for them. Since there was only about a gunny
sack full, Clint didn't see where this was such a sacrifice
for the man to make, but he didn't say anything.

Tito Calhoun rode into Virginia City the day before Clint
and Morgan were scheduled to leave. He had answered
Tom Kent's telegram immediately with a simple reply of
"I'LL BE THERE."

Kent had no idea what Calhoun's attitude would be when he arrived. Would he be angry that he'd spent time in prison? Angry at Kent for being a lawman and part of that system? Happy to be out of prison? He knew he'd just have to wait until his one-time friend arrived.

Kent was seated in a chair in front of his office when Calhoun rode down the street on a worn-out looking dun. He rode right past the lawman without looking at him, which Kent had expected. They didn't want anyone to see them together. Calhoun also rode past the more expensive hotels in town and stopped at the far end, at a hotel that looked as if it would fall down with the first good wind that came along.

Kent got up from his chair, but when he stepped into the street, he went in the opposite direction, toward the house that Diane shared with her husband, Arliss Morgan.

All Tito Calhoun knew was that he'd received a telegram from Tom Kent asking him to come to Virginia City "for work." Since he was just out of prison and had no money, he decided to answer the call. He stole a horse and rode to town. By the time he arrived, the horse was stove in and ready to collapse.

"Here," Calhoun said, handing the liveryman the reins, "you can have it."

"Mister," the man said, "this horse ain't no good no more."

"I know."

"What do you want me to do with it?"

"I don't care," Calhoun said.

Calhoun knew the liveryman was judging him by his clothes, which were the same ones he'd had on when he was arrested three years ago. They were as worn as his holster and his gun. He needed to replace all of them. Maybe this job would enable him to do that.

They'd given him three dollars when he got out of prison.

He still had a dollar, enough for a meal but not a hotel room. Still, he'd checked into the cheapest hotel he could find. He figured when he took this job, Kent would pay for the hotel. Hopefully, he'd also pay for new duds and a new gun and rig.

"Don't you want the saddle?" the liveryman asked.

"Sure," Calhoun said, "keep it aside for me. You sell horses?"

"Yes, sir."

"I'll be back," Calhoun said.

He left the livery and went to his cheap hotel room. Run-down as it was, the bed was still better than what he had slept on for three years in Huntsville. He lay down on his back and waited.

Kent realized that Arliss Morgan was home, so there was no way he could get to Diane at that moment. Instead, he decided to perform his rounds, which eventually brought him to the hotel Calhoun had checked into.

"Got a stranger checked in today, Sheriff," the middle-aged clerk said.

"That a fact?"

"Looks like a hard case just got out of prison," the clerk said. "His clothes is all wore out."

"Guess I better see what he wants in Virginia City," Kent said. "Thanks, Orson."

"Sure thing, Sheriff."

Kent went upstairs and knocked on Calhoun's door.

SIXTEEN

Clint saw the man ride in and recognized the type immediately. The worn, stove-in horse and faded clothes—he looked like a man fresh from prison.

But Clint gave it no more thought than that.

When Calhoun opened the door, he saw Tom Kent standing in the hall.

"Look at the shiny badge," he said.

Kent didn't know what to make of that, but then Calhoun smiled and said, "Hello, Tom."

"Tito."

"Come on in."

He backed away and let the sheriff enter his room.

"Sorry it's so cheap," Calhoun said. "It was all I could afford. That's a lie. I can't afford nothin'. I got one dollar on me."

"Don't worry," Kent said. "I'll pay the bill."

"Even if I don't take the job?"

"I think you'll take the job, Tito."

Calhoun sat on the edge of the bed.

"With a dollar in my pocket, I guess that's a good bet.

What I'm wonderin' is . . . what's a lawman want with me? What kind of job do you have?"

"One that you're good at and I ain't, Tito," Kent said. "We're gonna rob somebody."

Calhoun scratched his nose, stretched his legs out and regarded the tips of his worn boots.

"You gonna be able to gimme an advance so I can buy some new duds? And a horse? And maybe a gun?"

"All of that."

Calhoun looked up at Kent.

"Then this is a big job you want done."

"It's a big job, but I don't only want it done. I'll be there with you."

"Just you and me?"

"I told you," Kent said. "This is what you know, not what I know. You'll have to tell me if just the two of us can do it."

"How much are we talkin' about?" Calhoun asked.

This was the delicate part. As soon as Kent told Calhoun how much was involved, he knew the outlaw would want half.

"I got another partner, Tito," he said carefully. "The money's gonna have to be split in thirds."

"What about if we have to hire some help?"

"That can come out of my end."

"So there's a lot of money involved," Calhoun said, with the emphasis on the word "lot."

"Yes," Kent said. "A lot."

"How much?"

Kent hesitated.

"Don't worry, Tom," Calhoun said. "I'm just out of prison, I'm gonna be happy with my end. Besides, we're friends. In my business you don't double-cross friends."

Kent still hesitated, but before Calhoun could speak again, he said, "Six hundred thousand dollars, give or take a thousand."   •

"Six hundred thou—" Calhoun frowned. The biggest haul he'd ever made had netted him six grand. Now he was being offered two hundred thousand.

"What the hell are we robbin'? A bank?"

"Kind of," Kent said. "It's a poker game with some bankers in it."

"A poker game?" Calhoun asked. "With that much money involved?"

"Yes."

Calhoun whistled. "I'm gonna need some information."

"I've got some," Kent said. "I'm gettin' the rest."

"How many players?"

"Six."

"Anybody else around?"

"Somebody's hostin' the game," Kent said. "Probably some security involved."

"I'll bet," Calhoun said. "Who are the players?"

"Not sure."

"If anybody like Bat Masterson or Luke Short is involved, we'll need more men."

Kent scratched his chin.

"Any of them involved?"

"Don't know yet."

"Do you know any of the players involved?"

"Well . . ."

"Come on, Tom," Calhoun said. "I need to know everything."

"Well, the banker in town was going to play, but now he's backin' another player."

"And who would that player be?"

"His name's Clint Adams."

"Well, hell," Calhoun said, "looks like we are gonna need some help, after all."

SEVENTEEN

Clint had supper with Arliss Morgan at the restaurant in the Stockman Hotel.

"A buggy?" Morgan asked, bristling. "Why? Because of my age?"

"I was concerned about you on horseback," Clint said. "Since you're the manager of a bank, I assume you spend a lot of time behind a desk."

Somewhat mollified that he wasn't being called too old to ride, Morgan said, "Well, you might have a point. I wouldn't want to slow us down."

"Any rough terrain where we're going?" Clint asked. "Something a buggy wouldn't be able to negotiate? Maybe we should get a buckboard instead? Something more solid."

"A buckboard would be a waste," Morgan said. "No, a buggy sounds good."

"Good," Clint said. "I'll check with the livery and see if they have one I can rent."

The waiter came with their steaks.

"I'm gong to enjoy this," Morgan said. "We'll be eating on the trail tomorrow night."

"Are you saying you're not going to like my bacon and beans?" Clint asked.

Morgan looked appalled.

"That's what we'll be having?"

"It's easy to carry," Clint said. "Don't worry, there'll be some good, strong trail coffee to wash it down."

"Well," Morgan said, "at least where we're going they'll have decent food."

"And where are we going?" Clint asked. "Or do you want to keep that to yourself until we get there?"

"No," Morgan said, "of course not." He cut into his steak, popped a chunk into his mouth and chewed it thoughtfully. Clint thought the man was trying to think of a reason not to tell him. He helped himself to some steak while Morgan chewed his.

"We're going to a ranch owned by a man whose name is John Deal. My friend Deal is very wealthy and loves poker."

"You said he played?"

"But not very well," Morgan said. "Actually, I was going to say not as well as I do, but you've already given me your opinion of how I play."

"Sorry."

Morgan waved a hand.

"That's okay. Don't worry about it. It just makes me a smart man for getting you to play in this game instead of me."

"Do you know any of the other players?"

"I know there are two men coming from Europe," the banker said. "One is English, the other German. Other than that I don't know anything."

"But the two foreigners," Clint said, "surely they're coming all this way to play themselves."

"That is my understanding."

"Good," Clint said.

"Why is that?"

"We only have to worry about three players bringing in outside talent," Clint said.

"And if that outside talent is someone you know?" Morgan asked. "A friend? Would that be a problem?"

"Hell, no," Clint said. "Poker's poker. There are no friends at the poker table."

"I'm glad to hear you say that."

They continued their meal in silence until Clint thought of another question. The banker obviously did not believe in the concept of chitchat.

Clint's question was prompted by the appearance of the man he'd seen ride into town. The change was startling. He was wearing new clothes and he'd had a shave and a bath. He sat down alone at a table and ordered a steak dinner.

"What's wrong?"

"You know that fellow?" Clint asked. "Sitting against the wall? Black hat."

Morgan looked.

"Never saw him before. You?"

"No," Clint said, "but I saw him ride into town today. He's eating in the most expensive place in town but earlier he was dressed like he was fresh from prison."

"You can tell such a thing from the way a man's dressed?" the banker asked.

"Oh, yeah."

"So what does that mean?"

Clint thought a moment, then said, "Nothing, really. Tell me, who else have you told where we're going?"

Morgan stared at him for a moment, then said, "No one."

"No one? At all?"

"No one," Morgan said again.

He's told his wife, Clint thought. At least his wife.

Morgan kept his eyes on his plate the rest of the meal, which only confirmed what Clint was thinking.

EIGHTEEN

After Clint and Arliss Morgan parted company in front of the Stockman, Clint wondered again about the stranger who had ridden in earlier in the day. Obviously, the man had come into some money. Or perhaps he simply had a bank account and had withdrawn money. There was a second bank in town.

Clint decided to put the man out of his head and go to the livery to arrange for a buggy for Morgan. He felt better about their one-day ride now that he didn't have to worry about the banker falling off his horse.

Tito Calhoun entered the livery, wearing new clothes, new boots and a new gun belt. The only thing he had on that he'd ridden into town with was his Peacemaker. That he had left in someone's care, and they had kept it clean for him. He was also fresh from a haircut and a shave.

As he entered, he saw the liveryman talking to another man, and they were standing next to a buggy. He'd seen the same man in the restaurant just a little while ago. But the first time he'd seen him was when he rode past one of the hotels coming into town. From Tom Kent's description, he thought he knew who the man was.

"You can pick yer horse from out back," the liveryman said.

Calhoun had intended to interrupt the two men, but now he decided to just wait and listen.

Clint saw the man as soon as he entered, and he no longer wanted to discuss his business.

"You can take care of this fellow," he said. "I'll go out back and have a look."

He needed one horse to pull the buggy, and it had to be a good one. He went out back to the corral to inspect the stock, hoping the liveryman would complete his business with the stranger and join him.

Clint Adams was obviously a careful man, Calhoun thought.

"Yer back," the liveryman said.

"Yep," Calhoun said. "I need to buy a horse."

"Got a corral full out back," the man said. "Other fella's lookin' for a horse to rent to pull a buggy. You can go out back and look at the same time."

"Thanks," Calhoun said. "I think I'll do that."

The back door to the barn opened and the liveryman—Clint thought he'd said his name was Pete—came through leading the stranger. Seemed like they were destined for a meeting, one way or another.

The two men came over to the corral, where Clint was already inside, examining the stock.

"Got another feller here lookin' fer a horse," Pete called out. "Only he's lookin' ta buy."

"Good for you," Clint said. He looked at the other man. "My name's Clint Adams."

"Calhoun," the man said. "Just rode in today."

"I know," Clint said. "I saw you."

"Saw you, too," Calhoun said. "Got business here?"

"Just passing through, really."

"Yeah, me, too. Know anybody in town?"

"Not before I got here," Clint said, "but I've met a few people. You?"

"Sheriff's an old friend of mine," Calhoun said. "Just thought I'd stop in and say hello. I've been . . . away a while."

Clint thought it was funny how men who had been in prison usually said the same thing.

Calhoun entered the corral and began to inspect the stock along with Clint. He seemed to know what he was doing. He keyed in on a five-year-old steel dust that Clint had given a look to and decided was too good to pull a buggy.

"Nice animal," Clint said as Calhoun ran his hands up and down the horse's legs. "You've got a good eye."

"Thanks. The right horse is important. The one I rode in on is a nag."

Clint didn't comment. He knew Calhoun had either bought that one cheap or stolen it.

"I'll take this one," Calhoun told Pete. "Let's go inside and work on a price. And make it reasonable. I ain't about to haggle."

"Hagglin's part of horse tradin'," Pete said.

"I ain't tradin', I'm buyin'," Calhoun said, "and I ain't hagglin'."

He nodded to Clint, left the corral and headed back to the barn. Pete exchanged a look with Clint, who said. "Better come up with a fair price the first time."

Pete nodded and followed Calhoun.

NINETEEN

Pete eventually came back outside, where he and Clint agreed on a price to rent the buggy and the horse. An eight-year-old mare Clint felt was good enough for the job.

"How'd you do with that other fellow?" Clint asked.

"I give him a fair price and he took it," Pete said. "Easiest sale I ever made."

"What about a saddle?"

"Kept that old one he rode in on."

"And the other horse?"

"He give it to me, but it ain't good for nothin'."

"Did he say when he was leaving town? Or where he was going from here?"

"Nope," Pete said. "He just bought hisself a horse. Funny thing, though."

"What's that?"

"He asked me a lot of the same questions about you."

Clint decided to stop in on the sheriff after he finished up at the livery. The man looked up from his desk as Clint entered. From the look on his face he was expecting someone else.

"Adams," he said. "Can I do somethin' for you?"

"You've got a stranger in town named Calhoun."

Kent sat back in his chair.

"Yeah, I know about him."

"I just met him at the livery," Clint said. "Told me he was a friend of yours."

"More like an acquaintance, from years ago," Kent said. "I was surprised to see him here."

"You got any idea what he's doing here?"

"Just passin' through, as far as I know."

"You talked to him?"

"Of course I did," Kent said. "That's my job."

"He told me he was here to see you."

"I don't think that's true," Kent said. "Not entirely, anyway. But we did renew acquaintances, and I don't think he's gonna stay here more than a day."

"Looks to me like he might've just gotten out of prison."

Kent studied Clint for a moment, then said, "If he did, that's his business, ain't it? What's your interest?"

"With my reputation, it pays to keep tabs on some people," Clint said vaguely. "Thanks for your time."

"Speakin' of leavin' town," Kent said, "how much longer you figure on stayin'?"

"Not much," Clint said. "Don't know for sure yet, but not much longer."

"Well, enjoy the rest of your stay. I don't think you've got anything to worry about from Calhoun."

"Okay, thanks."

Clint walked to the door, then turned back.

"What's this Calhoun's first name?"

"Tito."

"Tito?"

"Mexican mother, Irish father," Kent said. "Why?"

Clint shrugged.

"Like I said, just keeping tabs."

He left the sheriff's office, then stopped just outside the

door. He had a feeling the lawman wasn't telling him every-thing he knew about Tito Calhoun.

But he thought he knew who could tell him more, and he headed for the telegraph office.

TWENTY

Now that Calhoun and Kent had established that they knew each other, it was no problem for Calhoun to enter the lawman's office soon after Clint had left.

"Adams was just here askin' about you," Kent said.

"So what?"

"What did you say to him?"

"Nothin'," Calhoun said, sitting across from Kent. "I just got to know him a little."

"You think that was smart?"

"He saw me ride in," Calhoun said. "We was both at the livery gettin' a horse. It woulda looked bad not to say somethin'."

"Maybe."

"He knows from my clothes and my horse that I just got out. Hell, he can tell. It still don't mean nothin'. Relax, Tom."

"Yeah, okay," Kent said.

"What'd you tell him?"

"Nothin'" Kent said. "I handled it okay. I told him we were acquainted."

"You're sure he's gonna be at this game?"

"He's playin' in the game," Kent said. "I got that for sure."

"We need to know who else is in that game," Calhoun said. "We can't make a move without knowing that. We don't know what we'll be walkin' in to."

"What if we just wait until the game's over and rob the winner?" Kent asked.

Calhoun shook his head.

"You think those fellas are gonna come out pattin' the winner on the back? Or that the winner's gonna be smiling and actin' like a winner? That ain't gonna work, Tom. We'd have to rob all of them just to find the winner."

"So what do we do?"

"We take the game while it's in progress," Calhoun said.

"You mean . . . we go in?"

Calhoun nodded.

"And that's why we have to know who is at that table," Calhoun explained. "And how many men we're gonna need. We can't walk into that room blind, and walk into a bunch of guns."

"I get it," Kent told him.

"Then get it," Calhoun said. "Get the information."

"I will."

"I've got some men standing by in Selwin," Calhoun said. Selwin was the next town over, going north. "We'll pick up however many we need on the way, but it's up to you to find out how many that is."

"All right," Kent said. "I'll find out. I told you I'd get all the information we need. But there's something you need to understand, too, Tito."

"What's that, Tom?"

"I'm in charge of this . . . expedition."

"Just call it a job, Tom," Calhoun said. "We're pullin' a job."

"Fine," Kent said, "it's a job, but it's my job. I put it together, so I call the shots. Do you understand that?"

Calhoun stared at Kent for a few moments, then said, "Hey, Tom, sure I understand. Listen, you gave me somethin' to do when I got out, you bought me new clothes, a new horse." He slapped Kent on the back. " 'Course I know you're in charge. I'm just tryin' to do what you brought me in to do."

"Okay," Kent said, "I just wanted to get that cleared up before we go any further."

"It's clear, boy," Tito Calhoun said. "Believe me, it's real crystal clear.

TWENTY-ONE

Clint knew there was a good chance he'd have to leave town before he got a return telegram from his friend Rick Hartman. But luckily, that turned out not to be the case. The telegraph operator found Clint standing at the bar in the Red Garter and handed him his reply.

"Whataya got there?" Dave Hopeville asked.

"Just a telegram answering some questions."

"About who?"

Clint refolded the telegram and picked up the beer he had been working on.

"You're pretty nosy."

"Guilty," Hopeville said. "I like to know what's going on in town."

"Well, this really isn't about the town," Clint said, "so there's no need to worry, or wonder."

"In other words, it's none of my business," Hopeville said without rancor.

"No," Clint said, "those are pretty much the words."

"I gotcha," Hopeville said. He turned to the bartender. "Charge him double for his beer."

"Right, Boss."

As Hopeville walked away, Travis leaned over the bar and said, "He don't mean it."

"I know," Clint said. "Give me another one, will you?"

It was an odd feeling for Diane to be with a man who didn't want to have sex with her, but it was actually a relief as well.

Tom Kent was all wound up—too much so, in fact, to be able to perform. When she grabbed his crotch, nothing happened, and he backed away.

"Something's on your mind," she said.

"I need the information, Diane," Kent said. "I can't plan anything until I know when, where and who."

"I've got the when and where," she assured him.

"You do?"

"I finally managed to pry it out of him."

"Well? Where is it?"

"A day's ride from here," she said. "A ranch owned by a man named John Deal."

"You're kiddin'," Kent said. "A poker game in the home of a man named Deal?"

"I'm not kidding," she said.

"And when is it?"

"It starts on Sunday," she said. "Arliss and Adams are leaving tomorrow."

"Okay," Kent said. "Okay. The game should go on for a few days. We've got plenty of time. Now all we need are the names of the players."

"I don't have that."

"Damn it, Diane—"

"Arliss doesn't have it, either," she told him. "They won't find out who all the players are until they get there."

"Exactly where is this ranch?" Kent asked.

"California," she said. "Between here and Sacramento."

"Sacramento," he said. "That's bad."

"Why?"

"Too much law there. It's a big city. Sheriffs, marshals and a police force."

"Why are you worried about that?" she asked. "You're not going to Sacramento after you hit the game."

"Well, we can't come back here, either."

"No," she said. "We'll meet in Sparks, and then head north to Oregon. They won't find us there."

"We hope."

She came closer and stroked his face, then stopped. She didn't want to get him worked up.

"Do you have your men set?"

"I'm workin' on it," he said. "We don't know how many we'll need."

"We?"

"I have one man already," Kent said. "He'll be my right hand. But without knowing exactly who's in the game, it will be hard to figure out how many men we'll need."

"It's bound to be a bunch of businessmen and gamblers," she said.

"Yeah," Kent said, "gamblers like the Gunsmith, maybe."

"He's only one man."

"Unless somebody like Bat Masterson or Ben Thompson is involved."

"Then take enough men to handle any eventuality," she said calmly.

"We'll have to pay them."

"You can get them cheap," she said. "All you need is enough guns to keep anyone from getting brave. If you get the jump on them—"

"Diane," he said, "leave the actual plannin' to me, okay? I'll do what I can with the information that you're givin' me."

Now she grabbed his face in her hands, and not in a way that could be misconstrued as romantic.

"Don't lose your nerve on me now, Tom Kent."

He backed off from her so that her hands fell away from his face.

"I'm not losin' my nerve, Diane," he said. "I want this money as bad as you do."

She doubted that.

"That's good," she said. "That's all I wanted to know."

"I have to go," he said. "I can't stay."

She considered pouting, but thought that might convince him to stay.

"I have to go, too," she said. "Are you going to leave tomorrow, like they are?"

"If the spread you're talkin' about is big enough, we'll probably be able to find it," Kent said. "If we try to follow them, we might be spotted."

"I'll try to pin the location down further for you," she said. "We can talk again in the morning, while Arliss is preparing to leave."

"Good," he said. "I'll see you in the mornin', then."

She decided she at least had to kiss him good-bye, just to keep him hooked. She did so, but made it short and kept her tongue to herself.

"In the morning," she said.

"I'll be here."

He left the hotel and went to meet Calhoun.

TWENTY-TWO

"I'm gonna follow them," Calhoun said.

They were in one of the smaller saloons in town, where they figured nobody would see them. It didn't really matter, but they didn't want to push their luck.

"What?"

"I'm not gonna take a chance that we can't find this place," the outlaw said.

"But you might be spotted—"

"Don't worry," Calhoun said. "I ain't been in prison so long I forgot how to trail somebody without bein' seen."

"Yeah, but this is the Gunsmith—"

"Relax, Tom," Calhoun said. "It's gonna be okay. I'll follow them, locate them and then get word to you."

"How are you gonna do that?"

"I'll take somebody with me," Calhoun said. "Got the man all picked out. And before you ask, they won't spot him, either. Guaranteed."

Kent stared into his beer.

"You're gonna have to get rid of that badge," Calhoun said.

"What?"

"At least take it off when you're around me," the outlaw said. "It gives me the creeps."

Kent looked down at his badge, then slowly unpinned it and dropped it into his shirt pocket.

"When are you gonna resign?" Calhoun asked.

"I-I hadn't thought about it."

"Well, don't do it before the job," Calhoun said, "do it after."

"After?" Kent asked. "I, uh, didn't think I'd come back here after."

"You have to come back," Calhoun said, "or they'll know you were in on it. You have to come back and stay awhile."

"But . . . ain't they gonna see our faces?"

"I hope not," Calhoun said. "We're gonna wear masks. I figured you knew that."

"Oh, yeah . . . What about you?" Kent asked, to hide the fact that he hadn't known about the masks. "What are you gonna do after?"

"Me? I'm just gonna take off with my share."

"And what about my share?"

"I assumed your partner would hold it for you."

"My partner?"

"You said somebody else was involved," Calhoun said with a shrug. "Somebody who was givin' you the inside information. I assumed they'd hold it."

"Oh, yeah, right."

"Don't you trust them?"

"Sure I do."

"Then there's no problem, right?" Calhoun asked. "You should probably come back, stay six months and then resign."

"Six months!"

"Or three, or nine," Calhoun said. "It's up to you. Now, about the players' names . . ."

"That was the only piece of information I couldn't come

up with," Kent said. "Nobody knows. They won't know until they get there."

"That's gonna make things a little harder."

"But not impossible."

"No," Calhoun said. "We'll just have to go in fast and hit them hard, before anybody can make a move. Tom . . . we'll have to kill them all. You got a problem with that?"

"Kill them? But why?" Kent asked. "You just said we'd be wearin' masks."

"That was when I thought we'd know who and what we were up against," Calhoun said. "If we don't know who's in that room, we're gonna have to go in with guns blazin'. When I identify the players, I want them to be dead."

"You . . . got men in mind who'll do that?" Kent asked.

"Yeah, I do," Calhoun said. "We're gonna need maybe six good men. With us that'll make eight."

"You ain't thinkin' about an eight-way split, are you?" Kent asked. Diane wouldn't stand for that.

"No, no," Calhoun said. "Me and you are the only ones gettin' an even split."

"And my partner."

"Right, right," Calhoun said, "and your partner. The others will just be guns for hire. We'll pay them before we split the take three ways."

"Why before?"

"That way it don't all come out of one person's cut."

"You've got this all thought out, don't you?"

"Most of it," Calhoun said. "Some of it's just the way things are done when you're dealin' with a gang."

"A gang . . ."

"Your gang, Tom," Calhoun said. "The Kent Gang."

TWENTY-THREE

Diane rolled over in bed and looked at the naked man lying next to her. He was lying on his back with his hands behind his head, and his impressive erection was pointing at the ceiling. She reached over and took it in one hand, began to stroke it. She was amazed at the hardness of it, since she had just finished riding it only ten minutes ago.

"You're an amazing man," she said.

"Because of that?" he asked, looking down at his own penis. "Lady, I tol' you, I been in prison."

"I know what you told me, Mr. Calhoun," she said.

"You got hold of my tallywhacker, Mrs. Morgan. I think you can call me Tito."

"Mmm, yes, I do have a hold on you," she said, pumping harder with her hand. "I think it was a lucky thing for both of us that you followed Tom when he met with me today."

"And then invited you to my room?"

"Yes," she said. "Only it was lucky I waited and didn't run into him here."

"I knew he had a partner," Calhoun said. "I wanted to find out who it was. Imagine how surprised I was when it turned out to be a woman—and a beautiful one, at that."

"Beautiful," she said, "as well as smart and hungry."

"Yeah," he said. "That, too."

She released his cock and ran her hand over his chest, stopping at each scar.

"Did you get these in prison?"

"Some in prison, some before," he said.

She touched one. "What's this from?"

"Bullet."

"And this one?"

"A knife."

"And this?"

"A bigger knife."

She touched his side, which had three puckers in it, equidistant from each other.

"And this?"

"A pitchfork."

"Ouch," she said. She leaned over and kissed the largest of the scars. "You must be a hard man to kill."

"I am," he said, "and I'm a hard man to control. I'm not Tom Kent, or your husband."

"I know that." She slid her hand down between his legs again and stroked his heavy testicles.

He grabbed her by the wrist. "So if we do this," he said, "you're not callin' the shots. I am."

"I've been waiting for a man to come along and call the shots," she said.

"I thought Tom was your man."

"I thought Tom was your friend."

"I ain't friends with no lawman."

"But if he does this—"

"I sure as hell ain't friends with a crooked lawman," he said, cutting her off. "He's provin' he's not a man to be trusted."

"And you are?"

"Yeah," he said, "I am. If I say I'm gonna do somethin', I do it."

"So you'll kill Arliss, and all of the other men in the game, and then you'll kill Tom?"

"I'd kill anybody who gets in my way."

"Even me?"

"Even you."

She moved quickly, straddling him, trapping his erect penis beneath her.

"When you called for me at that other hotel today, I knew you were the man for me."

"How did you know that?"

"Because you're the only real man I've ever met," she said. "When you opened the door of your room and I saw you standing there, I had to get my clothes off as fast as I could."

"Did you ever tell Tom Kent the same thing?"

"Tom Kent was a means to an end," she said.

"Huh?"

"Darling," she said, stroking his chest, "I was supposed to meet him so I could meet you. It was fate."

He reached down, lifted her by the hips so that his penis could ride up again, then brought her down on him, impaling her.

"That feel like fate?" he asked.

She laughed and said, "It feels like you're going to fuck me silly again."

"You got a dirty mouth for a woman."

"You don't like it?" She rose up and came back down on him, taking him all the way into her steaming depths.

"You crazy?" he asked, reaching for her breasts. "I love it!"

TWENTY-FOUR

Clint rolled away from the sleeping, naked woman in his bed, stood up and walked to the window. He'd only felt he could keep up with one woman tonight, not two. He let the women decide who that would be, so Loretta was sleeping in his bed at the moment. It was nice to be in demand with two civilized women who were willing to share.

He thought about what he'd agreed to do, play in this big game with gamblers from around the world. Certainly one of his friends Bat Masterson or Luke Short would have been better suited to this. Even Ben Thompson. But the fact was he'd walked into this, and the curiosity level was too high for him not to do it. He'd played in some high-stakes game before, but nothing to match this.

"Clint?"

He turned and looked at the girl on the bed. She was naked, propped up on one elbow.

"Come back to bed," she said. "I'm cold."

He was kind of cold, too. He went back to bed, took her in his arms and they fell asleep while keeping each other warm.

Clint rose the next morning and left the room without waking Loretta. They'd already said their good-byes. He took all his gear, because he doubted he would be returning to Virginia City.

He left the hotel and walked to the livery. When he got there, he was surprised to find the banker, Arliss Morgan, already there, the horse hitched to the buggy.

"What took you so long?" Morgan asked.

"You're very anxious to get going, aren't you?"

"You bet," Morgan said. "I would have saddled your horse, but I couldn't get near him."

"Yeah, he's temperamental sometimes. I'll saddle him and be right with you."

"I can ride over to the general store and pick up our supplies," the man offered.

"It's better if we do everything together from now until we get to the ranch," Clint said.

"You think somebody would try something?"

"You're carrying a lot of money, aren't you?"

"Well, actually, no . . ."

"I thought you told me a banknote wouldn't work."

"Actually, our host is arranging to have something set up so that we can all get the money we need rather easily."

Clint squared up and stared at the banker.

"Is there anything else you haven't told me yet?"

"I don't think so."

"Why was it so important to hold back that little bit of information?"

The banker actually shrugged, looked as if he'd just been scolded.

"Look, just wait here while I saddle my horse," Clint said. "Don't do anything, and don't go anywhere. Somebody is sure to know where we're headed, and they won't know that you don't have a bunch of money with you."

"All right."

Clint turned to go inside, then turned back and pointed his finger at the banker.

"Once we're on the trail, you're going to have to do

what I tell you to do, when I tell you, without question," he explained. "Is that understood?"

"Understood," Morgan said.

Clint went into the livery . . .

"Get away from the edge!" Tom Kent hissed.

Looking down at the livery from the roof of the building across the street, Tito Calhoun said, "They're not gonna look up here."

"They might."

"Relax, Tom."

"And how are you gonna get down from here fast enough to follow them?"

"We just have to see what direction they take when they leave," Calhoun said. "I'm not gonna be right on their trail, Tom. They'd see me for sure."

"What about this other fella you said was gonna help you track 'em?"

"I'll be catchin' up to him outside of town."

"Maybe I should go with you."

"You leave when we planned," Calhoun said, "in a few hours. You head for Carson City and pick up the rest of the men there."

"I don't know if this is gonna work."

"It'll work," Calhoun said. "We know the general area the ranch is in, and they're gonna be there for days."

Kent wasn't sure that Diane was going to be happy with this plan.

Tito Calhoun, on the other hand, had seen Diane happier than Kent had ever seen her, and just the night before. Running into a woman like Diane Morgan fresh out of prison was something Calhoun had not expected. He intended to enjoy her as much as possible, and use her to get ahold of the money. But he had no intention of sharing the money with Kent, Diane or any of the other men involved, except maybe for one. His intention was to use this money to make sure he never went to prison again.

He'd learned a valuable lesson in Huntsville Prison. No matter how tough you think you are, prison will wear you down and kill you, if you're there long enough. Luckily, his stretch was short—this time. But he thought if he ever went to prison again he'd probably die there. So he would do whatever he had to do, to whoever he had to do it to, to make sure that never happened.

But Diane Morgan . . . well, she'd be the last one he killed. He'd been without a woman for too long to dispose of this one too soon.

TWENTY-FIVE

Clint saddled Eclipse and walked him back outside, where Morgan was waiting. They then went over to the general store to pick up the supplies he'd ordered. Now that they had the buggy, they probably could have carried more, but Clint decided to stick with what he'd bought—coffee, beef jerky, some beans and bacon and cans of peaches.

As Clint stowed the supplies, Morgan, dressed in a banker's version of trail clothes—which meant he could have worn them to church on Sunday—stood by and asked, "Is there any way we could make it to the ranch tonight?"

"Not if it's where you told me it is," Clint said. "Better to spend one night on the trail. Why?" He turned to face the man. "When's the last time you slept on the ground?"

"To tell you the truth," Morgan said, "I don't think I've ever slept on the ground."

"Then it's probably a good thing you're not trying to ride, as well," Clint said. "One new experience at a time should be enough. Ready?"

"Uh, sure, I guess," Morgan said.

He walked around and climbed into the buggy while Clint mounted up.

"Are you armed?" Clint asked.

"I have a thirty-two-caliber Colt in a shoulder holster," the banker said. "I usually only wear it when we're transporting large sums of money."

"Can you shoot?"

"I can hit what I aim at, at close range."

"Okay," Clint said. "If we get into a shooting situation, you'll wait for word from me."

"Understood."

"Are we ready to go?" Clint asked. "You've said goodbye to your wife?"

"Oh, yes," Morgan said. "That's all taken care of."

"Does she know where you're going?"

"She knows I'm going to a poker game," Morgan said, "and that a lot of money is involved."

Clint studied the man. He knew when Morgan was bluffing at the poker table, and he knew now the man was lying. He was going to have to act on the assumption that Diane Morgan knew every detail, and go from there.

From his office window Tom Kent could see Clint Adams and Arliss Morgan loading their supplies onto the buggy. Kent wondered how much money Morgan had on him at the moment, and if it would be worth it just to ambush them for what the banker had on him. Given what Diane had told him about the amount of money involved, the banker must have had a hundred thousand dollars, at least.

That kind of money would last Tom Kent a lifetime. It would not, however, be enough for Diane Morgan.

Diane looked at the time on the grandfather clock in the sitting room of the house she shared with Arliss Morgan. If things went well, though, she would not be sharing it with him any longer. In fact, if things went the way she planned, she wouldn't even be seeing him again, ever.

Tito Calhoun had come into her life and transformed it. One afternoon with him and she knew that she was his sexual slave, and not the other way around, which is the way it usually went with men. She'd finally found a man who could enslave her. And not only that, he had modified her plan, making it even better. Rather than robbing the game and taking off with the money, she'd stay behind, become a wealthy widow and then sell off everything her husband owned. After that, she'd meet up with Calhoun. Between Arliss Morgan's personal fortune and the money they picked up from the game, she and Calhoun would be millionaires.

Millionaires!

That she had never planned on. It had taken Tito Calhoun to come up with that plan, and that's because he was a real outlaw, and not a wannabe like Tom Kent.

A real man and a real outlaw. That was what she needed, and that was what she had.

Finally, things in her life were going to go her way!

Tito Calhoun had sent Kent away because the man was driving him crazy. He thought he might have to kill him before the job just to shut him up.

He watched from the roof as Clint Adams and the banker left the livery and went to the general store. Tito had chosen this vantage point because he could see both structures very easily. While he watched, they loaded their supplies, had a discussion, then climbed aboard their buggy and horse and started west.

Calhoun had his horse saddled and ready behind the building. He got down from the roof, mounted up and slowly rode out of town. He had to pick up Dave Coffin—the other man he thought he might split his take with—outside of town. Dave was camped to the north. But he wanted to give Adams and Morgan a good head start anyway, and then track them. That gave him the time he needed to pick up Dave.

Dave Coffin was the only man he knew he could count

on: uneducated, loyal and good with a gun. Coffin had laid low the entire time Calhoun was in prison, but once he was out, Dave was ready to go. As soon as Calhoun heard from Kent, he had sent a telegram to Dave.

Tom Kent could never be a Dave Coffin. He'd spent too many years wearing that star, and whatever potential Kent may have shown years ago, whatever edge he may have had, that little hunk of tin had smoothed off of him long ago. Calhoun didn't even think Kent was going to be able to go through with this. The man was going to balk at some point, and that was probably when Calhoun was going to have to put a bullet into him.

TWENTY-SIX

Dave Coffin sat at the fire and poured himself another cup of coffee. When he heard the sounds of an approaching rider, he dumped the contents of the coffee cup into the fire and stood up, right hand hovering above his gun. When he saw the rider and recognized him as Tito Calhoun, he relaxed.

"Pour me a cup," Calhoun said, reining in his horse.

"We got time?"

"We got time," Calhoun said, tying off his horse, "but not a whole lot."

"Enough for you to tell me what this is all about?" Coffin asked. "You go away for a few years, then you get out and I hear from you out of the blue. Camp north of Virginia City and wait for you? What kinda telegram was that?"

"The kind that got you here, I guess."

Calhoun accepted the cup of coffee with one hand and shook his compadre's hand with the other.

"Long time, amigo," Coffin said.

"Too damn long," Calhoun said. "Good to see you, Dave. Hunker down here and I'll tell you what we're into."

"As long as we're into somethin'," Coffin said. "I been laying low way too long."

"I think you're gonna find it was worth the wait."

* * *

"Are we being followed?" Arliss Morgan asked as Clint
turned in his saddle once again.

"Not that I can see," Clint said, "but I keep checking."

"Adams, I've got to be honest with you."

"Never thought I'd hear those words from a banker or a
gambler," Clint said good-naturedly, "let alone from a man
who is both."

"I told my wife where I'm going and what we're doing,
and no one else," Morgan said.

"That wasn't such a good idea, Mr. Morgan."

"I trust her," Morgan said. "And you yourself have said
there's no one following us."

"That doesn't mean there's not a plan afoot somewhere."

"She'd never do that," Morgan said.

"Excuse me, Arliss," Clint said, "but I understand your
wife is quite a few years younger than you."

"Yes," Morgan said. "About thirty."

"Now, don't take offense, but when I see a situation like
that I usually think the woman is after something."

"Like my money?"

"For one."

"If she wants my money, she can have it," Morgan said.
"I love her."

Clint didn't like the look on the man's face.

"How much money are we talking about?"

"What?"

"Your personal worth, Mr. Morgan," Clint said. "Just how
much is it?"

"I don't see how that—"

"You're broke, aren't you?"

"Wha—"

"Don't try to bluff me, Arliss," Clint said. "I've already
proved I can read you."

Morgan was silent for a few moments, just the sounds of

their horses' hooves audible, and then he said, "I have had some financial setbacks."

"And does your wife know about those?"

"No."

"And are you broke?"

"I'm . . . cash poor."

"So all you've got is your property?"

"That's right."

"Where'd you get the hundred thousand to put up for this game?"

"I borrowed it."

"Where'd you get the money you're supposed to pay me?"

"I have enough money to pay you, Clint," Morgan said, "and if you win, there'll be plenty more. You know that."

"Oh, I know I'm going to do my part," Clint said. "It's your part I'm worried about."

"I'll do my part," Morgan said. "Believe me, I've been both rich and poor many times before."

"Well," Clint said, "to tell you the truth, I've never been either. I've always been somewhere in the middle, and that has suited me just fine. I'm not doing this for the money."

"Well, I'm not, either," Arliss Morgan said, then added, "Completely."

TWENTY-SEVEN

"Trail," Coffin said, pointing to the ground. "With the buckboard this is too easy."

They fell in behind the trail Clint Adams and Arliss Morgan were leaving.

"How are we gonna signal the others?" Coffin asked.

"They're only supposed to be going a day's ride," Calhoun explained. "Once we pinpoint where they're goin', you'll ride back and collect the rest."

"Where?"

"They'll be in Carson City," Calhoun said. "You find the nearest town with a telegraph and send one there to Tom Kent. He and the other men will then ride hell-bent for leather to here, and we'll take the game."

"What if it takes too long?" Coffin asked. "What if the game ends sooner than you think?"

"Believe me," Calhoun said, "a game like this will go on for days. We'll have plenty of time."

"I thought we knew where they were going."

"We know the rancher's name," Calhoun said. "We don't have the exact location."

"Well, why don't we just stop in some towns on the way

and ask?" Coffin suggested. "A ranch that size, somebody in a nearby town's gonna know how to get there."

"See?" Calhoun said. "I knew my brain was rusty from bein' inside and you'd come in handy."

"Then once we find out, we send a telegram and we're ahead of the game."

"That's fine with me. In fact, let's hit the next town."

"And what's the split gonna be?" Coffin asked. "You said we'd talk about it on the way."

"The split is gonna be you and me."

"You're gonna double-cross your friend Kent?"

"He ain't my friend," Calhoun said. "He's a lawman gone rogue."

"You can't trust a man like that."

"I know it."

"And what about your partner back in Virginia City?"

"It's a woman," Calhoun said. "The banker's wife. I'll hang onto her for a while. After all, I was in prison a long time."

"Can't blame you for that. What about the other men?"

"We'll just pay them off for a day's work. They never have to know how much is on the line."

"And if they find out and want a full share?"

"Then we'll give them a full share of lead," Calhoun said. "That sit right with you?"

"Long as I get my share, that's all I care about."

"You'll get your share. You got my word."

"Good enough for me."

They rode in silence for a while, and then Calhoun asked, "But why?"

"Why what?"

"Why is my word good enough for you? I mean, if I'm willin' to double-cross everybody else, why wouldn't I double-cross you?"

"Because we're the same, you and me, Tito," Coffin said.

"We got to have somebody we can count on. We kill each other, then what do we got?"

"You had that answer quick enough."

"Well," Coffin admitted, "I was considerin' double-crossin' you and takin' all the money for myself, but then I decided against it."

"When did you get so honest?"

"While you were inside," Coffin said. "Don't worry, it'll wear off."

TWENTY-EIGHT

They camped in a clearing with good visibility all around them. Clint quickly realized he'd have to do all the work in camp, but he figured he was getting paid enough for it. Once he had the horses bedded down, he made a fire and cooked their supper. All the while the banker was trying to find a comfortable rock to sit on.

Clint prepared the bacon and beans and handed a plate of them to Morgan, along with a cup of strong trail coffee.

"By God!" Morgan said after his first sip of coffee.

"It takes getting used to," Clint said. "If you don't like it, just drink water."

"No, no," Morgan said, "I just wasn't ready. It's both hot and strong."

The banker took a forkful of bacon and beans and shoveled it into his mouth.

"How's that?" Clint asked.

"Actually not bad," the banker said. "Not bad at all. It's not a steak at the Stockman, but . . ."

Clint thought the man was taking the change in his diet very well.

"And it is only for one night," Morgan added.

"Yes, it is."

When it came to sleeping, though, Morgan had more of a hard time.

"My God, how do you sleep on the ground?"

"I usually use my saddle as a pillow," Clint said. "Would you like to try?"

"No, thank you."

"It's a mild night," Clint said. "You could use your blanket as a pillow."

The banker tried that, but it didn't work either.

"Why don't you try sleeping on the buggy seat?" Clint asked. "At least there are springs there."

"That sounds like a good idea."

Morgan stood up, took his blanket and his gun and headed for the buckboard.

Before he climbed up, he asked. "Aren't you going to sleep?"

"I'm going to stand watch for a while," Clint said, "just in case."

"All night?"

"Maybe just till daylight."

"That's not fair," the banker said. "If you were traveling with someone else, wouldn't you split it up?"

"Well, yes, but—"

"I will do my share, Clint," Morgan said. "Wake me when you want to go to sleep."

Clint was going to argue at first, but then he decided to go along with it.

"All right, I will," Clint said. "Thanks."

"After all," Morgan said, "if anyone is after us, you're the one who is going to keep us alive, right? You'll need some rest."

"You have a point," Clint said. "Okay, then, get some rest and I'll wake you."

"Good night, then."

"'Night."

Clint hunkered down by the fire and prepared another pot of coffee.

In another camp Dave Coffin accepted a cup of coffee from Tito Calhoun and said, "If we rode at night, we could catch up to them."

"We don't want to catch up to them," Calhoun said. "We want them to get where they're goin'."

They had stopped in one small town where no one had ever heard of a rancher named John Deal. In the morning they'd try the town of Frankford, which was only a few miles ahead.

"You know, there's somethin' about that name," Coffin said.

"Which one?"

"Deal."

"What about it?"

"Sounds phony."

"You mean, like an alias?"

"Yeah."

"Why do you say that?"

"A bunch of bigwigs goin' to play poker at a ranch owned by somebody named Deal. Come on!"

"Coincidence."

"I just don't like coincidences," Coffin said. "I never have, and I never will."

TWENTY-NINE

When Clint woke in the morning, he could see Arliss Morgan sitting at the fire, trying to keep his head up and his eyes open. The fire was still going, though, and there was the smell of fresh coffee in the air.

He approached the fire and startled the man.

"Oh, good morning," Morgan said, rubbing his face. "I made fresh coffee."

"I can smell it," Clint said. "Why don't we just have this and then get moving? We should be there by afternoon."

"Suits me," the man said. "I'm going to appreciate a bed after only one night on the trail. I don't know how you do it."

"You get used to it," Clint said. "Some nights the sky is so beautiful I wouldn't want to sleep anywhere else."

"Well, I don't think I could do it," Morgan said. "Do you know that after you told me not to stare into the fire it took all my willpower not to do so?"

"That's human nature," Clint said. "Somebody tells you not to do something, your first instinct is to do it."

"You're an intelligent man, Clint," Morgan said. "That's not something that comes across in your reputation."

"It wouldn't," Clint said. "A man with a reputation for being smart isn't very interesting."

They finished their coffee, broke camp, and then Clint hitched the horse to the buggy and saddled his own.

As they rode along, Clint asked, "This fellow we're going to see. John Deal?"

"Yes?"

"That his real name, or am I in for a surprise?"

"It's his real name, as far as I know," Morgan said. "As to whether or not you're in for a surprise, I would bet the answer to that would probably be yes."

"The other players, you mean?"

"I mean who the other players might get to represent them," Morgan said.

"And what about me?"

"What about you?"

"Will I be a surprise to anyone?"

"Good Lord," the banker said, "I hope so."

"John Deal?" the man said. "Of course I've heard of him. He's a big rancher got a spread over near Sacramento."

Calhoun and Coffin both looked at the bartender.

"How close to Sacramento?"

"Well, it's actually outside of a town called Gardner," the barkeep said. "But you can't miss it, it's huge."

"What's the brand?" Coffin asked.

"Double-D."

"Why double?" Calhoun asked.

The bartender shrugged. "I guess you gotta ask Mr. Deal."

"You know what?" Calhoun said. "We will. Much obliged for the information."

As they stepped outside the saloon, Coffin said to Calhoun, "What's gonna happen when the game gets hit and this fella remembers talkin' to us?"

Calhoun looked behind them at the batwing doors.

"You got a point," he said. "Maybe we should stick around town just a little longer."

"And maybe not," Coffin said. "It's early and there's nobody else in there. You go and send your telegram, I'll go back inside, and then we'll get outta town."

"Okay," Calhoun said. "But be quick about it—and quiet."

"Oh," Coffin said, "I'll be quiet . . ."

Calhoun went to the telegraph office and sent off a missive to Tom Kent in Carson City. It was simple: "MEET ME IN GARDNER AS SOON AS YOU CAN." When he left the telegraph office, he hoped Kent was smart enough to know he meant Gardner, California.

"Here's your telegram, Sheriff," the telegraph operator said to Kent. "Finally came in."

This was the fourth time that morning that Kent had stopped in to check.

"Thanks."

"Must be real important."

"It is." Kent started to leave, then turned back. "Did you read it?"

The clerk smiled and said, "You know, I been on this job so long I can take the messages without even reading them." He pointed with his pencil. "I couldn't even tell you what that said."

Kent believed him.

Over in the Dry Gulch Saloon—one of the smaller ones in Carson City—Kent found the other four men waiting for him. Somehow Tito Calhoun had managed to hire these jaspers, either from Virginia City or before he even came there.

The spokesman of the four seemed also to be the oldest. His name was Alex Ruger.

"Time to go, finally?" he asked Kent as the man entered.

"Yes, it's time. Let's mount up."

"Where are we goin', exactly?" Ruger asked.

"I'll tell you along the way."

Kent started to leave, but the four held back.

"What is it?"

"We was all wonderin' if you was gonna wear that badge the whole time," Ruger said.

"Why?"

"Kinda makes us nervous."

Kent looked down at the tin star. He'd kept it on so that the telegraph operator would give him more attention. Now that the telegram had arrived, there really was no reason to wear it. But did he just want to toss it away?

He thought a moment, then unpinned it and dropped it into his vest pocket.

"I won't be wearin' it anymore," he told them.

"Then why keep it?" Ruger asked.

"I'm not," Kent said. "I'm gonna drop it somewhere along the trail."

"Sounds like a good idea," Ruger said.

"You boys ready to ride now?" Kent asked.

"We're ready," Ruger said.

After the sheriff left the telegraph office, the clerk took out the copy he always made of telegrams, just in case. He read it, didn't understand what it meant beyond what it actually said, and then dropped it into a drawer. He'd hold onto it for a little while, then discard it and a bunch of others.

What he'd told the sheriff was true enough. He didn't remember telegrams after he took them down. He did keep the copies for a while, though.

Just in case.

THIRTY

Clint was impressed with the spread owned by John Deal. They knew exactly when they were on his land, because they were approached by three armed riders, all wearing trail clothes, all in their midthirties to late thirties.

"Hold up, there," one of them shouted.

"Rein in," Clint said to Morgan. As the riders approached, Clint said, "You do the talking, since you're the one who was invited."

"Right."

"What are you gents doin' on Mr. Deal's land?" the man asked. "This is Double-D property."

"My name is Arliss Morgan," the banker said. "I've been invited by Mr. Deal."

"And him?" the man asked, jerking a thumb at Clint.

"He's been invited by me."

"What's his name?"

"Why don't you ask him?" Morgan said.

"What about it, friend?" the man asked. "You got a name?"

"Clint Adams."

"What?" the man asked, as if he wasn't sure he'd heard right the first time.

"My name is Clint Adams."

The three men exchanged glances, and then the leader looked at Arliss Morgan again.

"You got a gun, sir?"

"I do."

"I'll have to ask you for it."

Morgan looked at Clint, who nodded. The rider came up close to the buggy. Morgan took the gun from his shoulder rig and handed it over. Then the rider looked at Clint.

"Don't even think about asking for my gun," Clint said, cutting the man off at the pass.

Again the men exchanged glances.

"We're supposed to ask for everyone's gun, Mr. Adams," the leader said.

"Not mine."

"Well . . . okay," the man said. "I'll probably lose my job, but we'll take you in."

"I'll see that you don't lose your job, son," Morgan said.

"I'd be obliged for that, sir," the man admitted.

"This way."

The three riders rode up ahead and Clint and Morgan fell in behind them.

"That went well," Morgan said.

"Are you going to introduce me when we get into the house, or just have me introduce myself?"

"I thought I'd introduce you."

"Then why didn't you do that just now?" Clint asked. "Why'd you have me do it myself? To impress them?"

"Well, these were men with guns," Morgan said. "I thought— Did I do something wrong? Offend you?"

"I asked you to do the talking," Clint said. "That was all."

"All right," the banker said, "when we get inside I'll introduce you. You won't have to say a word."

"Cat's out of the bag now," Clint said. "Those men will pass the word, and I'm sure our host will hear it before we can even get to the front door."

"I'm sorry," Morgan said. "I thought I was making our way easier."

"It never pays to give away too much too soon," Clint said. "That's all I'm saying."

"I'll remember."

Too damn late now, Clint thought.

THIRTY-ONE

The three men all dismounted when they reached the house, a three-story structure painted all white. One of them took the buggy, the other took Eclipse to the livery. The leader said, "Wait here," and went into the house. He came back with a white-haired, fit-looking man in tow.

"My name is John Deal," he said with a British accent. "You are Arliss Morgan?"

Morgan stepped forward and said, "That's right."

Deal stuck out his hand.

"Happy to meet you. You and your companion are actually the first ones to arrive."

"We're not early—"

"No, no, merely prompt," Deal said. "And your friend, Mr. . . ."

"Adams," Arliss Morgan said, "Clint Adams."

"Yes, that was what my man told me," Deal said. "I was . . . puzzled as to why you would feel the need to bring . . . well, is he a, um, bodyguard?"

"Not at all," Morgan said. "Mr. Adams is going to play in my place."

"Oh, I see," John Deal said. "Well, Mr. Adams, welcome to my home." He put his hand out again and Clint shook it.

"I'm sure your presence will add some excitement and—shall we say spice?—to the game."

Clint studied Deal as they shook hands. As far as he could see, the man was who he said he was. Clint wasn't seeing anyone else beneath the white hair. John Deal seemed to be simply who he said he was, and no more.

"Please, follow me and I'll show you to your quarters."

They followed him up the stairs and into the house, Clint carrying his saddlebags and Morgan a small carpetbag.

From the man's ramrod-straight stature and his use of the word "quarters," Clint assumed that he had been in the military at some time.

They followed him through the front door and found themselves in a large entry hall. Clint wondered if Deal had built the house, or if he had bought it.

A middle-aged woman with brown hair worn in a bun was standing in the entry hall. She was solidly built, wearing a simple housedress.

"This is my housekeeper, Mrs. Pyatt," Deal said. "She runs my house and will see to all your needs. Mrs. Pyatt, will you show these gentlemen to their rooms? I believe you have one chosen for Mr. Morgan from Virginia City. Simply find Mr. Adams a room that suits him, please."

"Yes, sir. This way, gentlemen."

As they followed her up the stairs, her scent wafted down to them. Clint found it refreshing and wondered if it was just soap. Watching her from behind was not unpleasant. Although she was somewhat solidly built, Clint found her not unattractive. He thought if she tried, she could be very attractive.

They trailed behind her as she went down the second-floor hallway.

"Mr. Morgan, this will be your room."

"Thank you, Mrs. Pyatt."

"Please tell me if it is not satisfactory."

Morgan took a step inside, a quick look, and pronounced it very satisfying.

"Considering I had to sleep on the ground last night," he added, "it's marvelous."

"Thank you, sir. Mr. Adams?"

"I'll see you when I see you, Arliss," Clint said.

"That will probably be at dinnertime," Arliss said.

"Dinner, then," Clint said, and followed Mrs. Pyatt.

She took him to the end of the hall and another staircase.

"Since your arrival was not . . . anticipated," she told him, "I will have to give you a nook on the third floor."

"That's fine, Mrs. Pyatt."

"Follow me, then."

Once again he followed her solid, swaying behind up a flight of stairs. Here the scent was even more powerful. He thought about asking her what it was, but did not want to seem too forward with her.

"Here is your room," she said as they walked down the third-floor hall. "It is actually almost directly above Mr. Morgan's."

"Thank you, Mrs. Pyatt."

"Please let me know—"

Without stepping into the room, he said, "I'm sure this will be fine."

She appeared taken aback that he had cut her off, but she regained her composure very quickly.

"Dinner will be served promptly at six," she said, "in the dining room."

"Thank you."

She looked him up and down and sniffed. "If you would like a bath, it can be arranged."

"Actually," Clint said, "that sounds good."

"I'll have a girl come up and prepare your bath."

"That won't be—"

This time she cut him off.

"It is the way we do things, sir," she said.

"Well, then, Mrs. Pyatt," Clint said, "I'll . . . anticipate her arrival."

If she thought he was making fun of her, she gave no sign of it.

"Until dinner, then."

He watched her walk down the hall to the front stairs and then descend. When she was gone, he went into his room. It was easily larger and more luxurious then most hotels he had been in, but he was sure that it was not the same caliber as the room Arliss Morgan was standing in.

After all, his arrival had been anticipated.

THIRTY-TWO

Fresh from a hot bath, Clint decided to come down before dinner was served, thereby probably risking the wrath of Mrs. Pyatt. He decided to take a walk around outside for two reasons. One, he'd never been there before and he always liked to familiarize himself with new surroundings. And two, for the purposes of security for the game. He didn't know yet what part of the house the game would take place in, but he decided to walk around the entire house, and then check the grounds as well.

When he had circled the house completely, he walked over to the barn and entered. Inside he found a man unsaddling two horses, which had obviously just been ridden.

"More guests?" he asked.

The man turned quickly, saw Clint and relaxed. He was one of the three men who had ridden in with Clint and Arliss Morgan.

"Sorry," Clint said. "Didn't mean to startle you."

"I'm glad I recognized you," the man said. "If I'd gone for my gun . . ."

Neither of them wanted to think about what might have happened.

"Yeah, two more players got here a little while ago," the man said.

He went back to unsaddling the horse he'd been working on. The other mount stood by impatiently.

"Let me help you with that other one."

"Much obliged," the man said. "I ain't supposed to be handlin' horses."

"You know my name," Clint said. "What's yours?"

"Andy," the man said, "Andy Blevins."

"What's your job supposed to be, Andy?"

"Security."

"Inside and outside?"

The man shook his head.

"Outside, like we done with you."

"Do you know the names of the men who arrived after we did?" Clint asked.

"Naw," the other man said. "I don't get told no names if I ain't around when the question's asked."

"Like with me."

"Yeah."

"How many men are there working outside security?"

"Don't rightly know," the man said. "I heard a dozen, but I ain't never seen more than five or six at one time, myself. There's also ranch hands. I don't know what the whole payroll looks like."

"I met Mrs. Pyatt," Clint said. "She seems to rule the house with an iron hand."

"Ya gotta watch out for her," Andy said.

"Why's that?"

"Just watch out for her," he said. "Don't get caught alone with her. I don't wanna say no more."

Andy removed the saddle and blanket and began to rub the horse down. Clint was only seconds behind him.

"Okay," Clint said, deciding not to push it. Except for one question. "How long has she worked for Mr. Deal?"

"Longer than the rest of us," he said. "She came here with him when he bought the place."

"Bought it?" Clint asked. "I thought maybe he'd built it."

"Nope," Andy replied. "He bought it off of Mr. Stevenson last year."

"And did you work for Mr. Stevenson?"

"No," Andy said. "Mr. Deal cleaned house when he bought it. Let everybody go, hired his own people."

"That when you got your job?"

"Nope," Andy said. "I got hired specially for this— whatever this gatherin' is. Don't rightly know. Heard it was a poker game, but don't know for sure." He stopped and looked at Clint. "What kind of poker game needs all this security?"

"A big one," Clint said.

"You here for that?"

"I am."

"You know how many players?"

"Half a dozen or so, I hear," Clint said.

"That ain't such a big game."

Andy went back to rubbing the horse down. Clint didn't bother telling him that in this case the word "big" had nothing to do with the number of players involved. He finished the second horse, then told Andy he'd see him around.

"Obliged for the help," Andy said. "Us security types gotta stick together."

Apparently, Andy assumed Clint had been hired for inside security. Clint hesitated, then decided not to disabuse the man of that notion.

THIRTY-THREE

Clint got back to his room without running into Mrs. Pyatt, and he got dressed for dinner. Arliss Morgan had provided the funds for him to buy a new suit, one that he would wear not only to dinner but to the game as well.

When he found the dining room after taking a couple of wrong turns, he found a long table set with ten places. He knew that didn't mean ten players, since he was playing and Morgan wasn't. The same situation probably existed in at least one or two other instances.

Already present at the table were the host, John Deal, the banker, Arliss Morgan, and Mrs. Pyatt hovering about.

"Ah, Mr. Adams," Deal said. "Please, do come and join us. Mrs. Pyatt, get Mr. Adams a drink, please."

"What would you like, Mr. Adams?" she asked. "We have many selections—"

"What would you advise, Mrs. Pyatt?"

"Mr. Deal has a very nice brandy he has imported from back East."

"Then that will do, thanks."

"Have a seat," Deal invited, then added, "anywhere you like."

Deal was seated at one end of the table—presumably

the head—and Morgan had taken the chair just to his right. Clint walked over and sat to the head's left, directly across from the banker.

"How is your room?" Deal asked him.

"It's excellent, thanks. You have a beautiful spread here."

"Ah, have you seen it?"

"Well," Clint said, "obviously not all of it. We saw what we could as we rode in, and then I went for a walk just before dinner. I noticed there were two horses in the livery."

"Yes, some of the others have arrived. They should be down for dinner shortly. We also had two gentlemen come in from Sacramento in a buggy."

"So there are six here?" Clint asked.

"Yes," Deal said, "but we set the table for more, just in case. Whoever does not arrive today will be here tomorrow. We're due to begin the game Sunday night, and continue to play until one player has all the money."

"That suits me," Morgan said.

Clint was about to agree when two more men entered the dining room, coming in together.

"Gentlemen, welcome," John Deal said. "Already seated at the table are Arliss Morgan, a banker from Virginia City, and his proxy, Clint Adams.

"And these are Mr. Arne Blom, a banker from Sweden, and Monsieur Philippe Marceau from Paris."

Clint assumed, since no profession preceded Marceau's name, that he was a gambler by trade.

"Monsieur Marceau is Mr. Blom's proxy. Gentlemen, please be seated."

The two newcomers each executed a small bow, and took seats across from each other, the Swede next to Clint and the Frenchman next to Morgan.

"Mr. Adams," Blom said, with just the slightest Swedish accent, "I have heard your name."

"As have I," Marceau said. His English had a heavy

French accent. "But I do not recall hearing your name in connection to poker. More as a—how do you say it—*légende*?"

"Legend," Arne Blom translated.

Clint had gotten the gist, but he said, "Thank you."

But Marceau kept trying.

"You are a—ah, *spécialiste*? With a pistol?"

"A specialist?" Clint asked.

"I believe Monsieur Marceau means an expert with a gun," John Deal said.

"In that case," Clint said, "yes, I'm an expert with a gun. And a legend? Probably, although I don't personally lay claim to that title."

"Ah, then this should be—how you say—*facile*? For me?"

"Easy," Deal said.

"*Oui*, easy."

"You think so?" Clint asked.

"But of course," Marceau said. "You are ze expert with ze gun, while I am ze expert with ze cards. Easy work. *Facile!*"

"You just keep thinking that, monsieur," Arliss Morgan said. "It will work in our favor."

"And other players?" Blom asked.

"One other upstairs," Deal said, "the others are arriving tomorrow, no doubt."

"And if they do not arrive?" Blom asked.

"We will begin without them."

"What about their money?" Morgan asked.

"All the money has been deposited," Deal said. "My banker will be here tomorrow to give each player his chips. If a player has not arrived, his money will be added to the prize."

"Equally distributed among the players?" Clint asked.

"That was one way we could have done it," Deal admitted, "but I decided to simply award it to the winner. That way each player still begins with one hundred thousand."

"That sounds fair, I think," Morgan said.

Fair, Clint thought, to the players who were already there. Then again, two of those players had come all the way from Europe and had arrived on time. Perhaps there should be a stiff penalty for late arrivals.

Mrs. Pyatt came into the room.

"Shall we serve, sir?"

"I believe we have one more guest, Mrs. Pyatt," Deal said, "but you may remove the other place settings."

"Yes, sir."

As she did so, he told the others, "There's one more gentleman upstairs, getting ready—ah, and here he is."

Clint turned his head and was startled to see one of the most famous gamblers in the West enter the room. Although why he was surprised, he didn't know. Dick Clark had owned gambling establishments in Dodge City and Tombstone, among other places. Still owned some in Tombstone, as well as nearby Bisbee, Arizona. So why would he not be involved in one of the biggest private games in the West?

THIRTY-FOUR

"Son of a bitch," Clint said, getting out of his chair. "Dick, how the hell are you?"

He approached the man with his hand outstretched, and Dick Clark took it and shook it enthusiastically.

"Clint Adams," he said. "It's been a while. What are you doin' here?"

"Being outclassed by you, apparently."

The smaller, more slender man slapped Clint on the back and said, "Not much chance of that."

Clint was about to reply when the Frenchman appeared at his elbow.

"Excuse," Marceau said, "but zis is Dick Clark? The famous gambler?"

"This is him."

Clint stepped back and allowed the Frenchman to introduce himself. He was infinitely more excited to meet Dick Clark than he had been to meet Clint Adams, whom he considered to be *facile*.

Clark joined the other men at the table, shaking hands with both bankers, Blom and Morgan. He chose to sit on Clint's side of the table, with Blom between them.

"Mrs. Pyatt," John Deal said, "you may have dinner served now."

"Yes, sir."

The dinner was delicious, but the men were more interested in the conversation than the food and drink. Clint was interested in hearing what was going on in France and Sweden, both with poker and with life in general. The Frenchman Marceau, on the other hand, wanted to hear about Dodge City and Tombstone and Abilene, and he wanted to hear about it from Dick Clark.

"He loves the famous gamblers of the Old West," Blom explained to Clint. "Bat Masterson, Luke Short, Ben Thompson. And Mr. Clark, there. He considers them all gods."

"Well, those others have something Dick doesn't have," Clint said.

"And what is that?"

"They've all been lawmen and can all handle a gun."

"And not Mr. Clark?"

"I can't recall Dick ever being in a fight, or picking up a gun," Clint explained. "His right-hand man, Billy King, usually handles all that for him. Dick is a true gambler, with no other interests on the side."

While he was talking with the banker Arne Blom, Clint could hear Arliss Morgan trying to pump John Deal for the names of the remaining three players. He also wanted to know if they'd be playing for themselves or bringing someone to play by proxy, as he had.

"I can't tell you that, Arliss," Deal said. "I did not even know that you were bringing Mr. Adams. But you know the rules. As long as the money is on deposit, you may bring anyone you like to play for you."

"I have a question," Clint said to Deal.

"Of course."

Everyone stopped talking in order to listen.

"Can the proxy be replaced by his backer at any time?" Clint asked.

"Only if the proxy must withdraw due to illness or injury," Deal said. "Otherwise only one player is allowed, from start to finish."

"Do you want to be replaced, Monsieur Adams?" the Frenchman asked. "Now zat you see Mr. Dick Clark and myself are here to play, eh?"

Before Clint could answer, Dick Clark cut in.

"If you think Clint is a soft touch because his main reputation is with a gun, Monsieur Marceau, you are sadly mistaken. Clint Adams is a first-rate poker player."

"Zis is true?" Marceau asked, looking around the table.

"I guess you'll just have to find out the hard way, Marceau," Arliss Morgan said.

Dick Clark looked chagrined, figuring he'd just given away an edge that Clint thought he had with the Frenchman. He gave Clint an apologetic look, which he simply waved away.

After dinner Deal asked all the men to accompany him to the den, where they could have more drinks and cigars.

On the way out, Dick Clark came up next to Clint and said, "Sorry about that. I thought he was running you down."

"It's okay," Clint said.

"He probably would have found out by the first hand, anyway," Clark said.

Clark walked ahead, and for the first time Clint thought that maybe the man hadn't given him away by accident at all. Maybe Dick Clark was looking for his own edge, giving the Fenchman the desire to see how well Clint could play. Maybe Clark was thinking he'd slip in there in the first few hands and get an early lead.

Gambler. Clint had enough friends in the profession to know they'd do anything to get an edge.

THIRTY-FIVE

In nearby Gardner, California, Tito Calhoun and Dave Coffin were sitting in a saloon, catching up on old times and planning what to do with the money from this new score.

"When are Kent and those other boys gettin' here?" Coffin asked. "Jesus, we could go in there tonight an'—"

It was the liquor talking and Calhoun had to rein Coffin in.

"The other players won't be there tonight," he explained, "and neither will the banker."

"Banker?"

"According to my source," Calhoun said, "they have a banker from Sacramento holding all the money, and he will also be there for the game—to give each player his stake."

"If we knew when that banker was coming," Coffin said, "and by what route, we could hit him before he got there."

"Yeah, but we don't," Calhoun said. "Kent and the others should be here tomorrow night, so we go day after tomorrow."

"So meanwhile we just sit here and wait?"

"No," Calhoun said, "we're gonna take a ride out there tomorrow and check on security, see how tight it is. We can either slip through or bust through. We'll have to decide which."

"I'd just as soon smash through 'em," Coffin said, his voice slurred.

"I know that," Calhoun said. "Why don't we turn in for the night?"

"Huh? The night's young. And you been in prison. Let's find some women."

"Well, then, how about you stop drinkin'?"

Coffin narrowed his eyes and stared across the table at his partner.

"You sayin' I can't hold my liquor?"

Calhoun leaned forward and said, "I'm sayin' you can't hold your liquor."

Coffin stared for a few moments, then burst out laughing so hard it drew the attention of the others in the saloon.

"By God, Tito, you're the only man who could say that to me and live."

"So you'll stop drinkin'?"

"No," Coffin said, still laughing, "but we can go and get somethin' to eat before we find some women."

Calhoun decided to take what he could get.

Camped somewhere between Carson City and Gardner, Tom Kent sat at the fire, drinking coffee while the other men slept. Two of them seemed to be competing to see who could snore the loudest, while the others occasionally leaned over and nudged them into silence.

Kent didn't like being separated from Tito Calhoun. For all he knew, Calhoun and his partner had already hit the game and were riding off with the money. He didn't know what had made him trust a man who had just gotten out of prison. Sure they'd known each other years ago, but they were not friends, not by any means.

He touched his pocket, where his badge still resided. He hadn't yet tossed it away. He took it out and held it in his hand, let the light from the fire reflect off it. He remembered how proud he'd been to wear his first sheriff's badge, after all the years of wearing a deputy's star. Now he was preparing to just chuck it away, for a woman and for some money.

Some money?

Six hundred thousand dollars was more than some money!

There could be no second thoughts when it came to that much cash.

He held the badge out over the fire, then let it drop from his hand into the flames.

THIRTY-SIX

After brandy and cigars in the den, Clint decided to call it a night and go to his room. He wanted to be well rested for the next day. As usual, he had a book in his saddlebags, and as usual it was Mark Twain. He'd decided to read everything the man had written, and this was a collection of Twain's short stories.

But before reading, he walked to the window, which overlooked the rear of the house. Below him he could see the glow of light from Arliss Morgan's room.

There was a knock on his door at that point. He had removed his gun belt and hung it on the bedpost, so now he drew the gun and carried it to the door.

"Who is it?"

"Don't shoot," Dick Clark said. "It's just me."

Clint opened the door, found Clark standing there alone.

"No more brandy and cigars?" Clint asked.

"I actually don't like brandy, and don't smoke cigars. Can I come in for a short chat?"

"Sure."

Clint backed away to allow Clark to enter, then closed the door. Clark looked at the gun in Clint's hand.

"They took my gun away when I got here."

"They tried," Clint said. He walked to the holster and slid the gun home. "What's on your mind, Dick?"

"I was wonderin' if you knew any more than I did about this game and the other players?"

"I don't know much," Clint said. "I didn't know you'd be here, but I did think this caliber of game might attract somebody I would know."

"Like Bat? Or Luke?"

"But seeing you is no surprise," Clint said.

"Well, seeing you is," Clark said. "I thought about that, too, but your name never came to mind. How did you end up here?"

Clint gave Clark the brief story.

"I guess I just couldn't resist," Clint said. "And there was always a possibility that all the players would be as bad as the one I had played. Now I can see that's not going to be the case."

"Have you ever heard of this Frenchman?"

"Never," Clint said, "but he seems very impressed with you."

"Too impressed," Clark said. "I think it's an act. He's a phony, and I think that'll come across in a very clear tell. We just have to find it."

"Well," Clint said, "we'll meet the rest of the players tomorrow. We'll know more then."

"I just wanted to check in with you, see if you had any insight you could give me."

"There's some insight I'd give you," Clint said, "and some I wouldn't, Dick."

Clark laughed and said, "That's fair enough, Clint."

They took a few moments to compare notes about mutual friends, then Clark said, "Well, I see a book on your bed. I'll let you get to it."

"Mark Twain," Clint said. "He goes everywhere with me these days."

"I can understand why," Clark said. "I've read him my-self."

Clint walked to the door with Clark, opened it for him.

"Oh, I did get a tip," Clint said, "but I don't know what it means, and I don't know how interested you'd be."

"Oh? What is it?"

"The housekeeper, Mrs. Pyatt." Clint said. "One of the hands warned me to not be alone with her."

"She looks harmless enough," Clark said. "And not un-attractive, I might add."

"Well, that's what I heard," Clint said, "for what it's worth."

"Interesting," Clark said, "but it has nothing to do with the game, so I'll set it aside."

"Good night, then."

"Good night. See you in the morning. I understand breakfast is at eight sharp."

"Kind of late for a working ranch."

"This fella Deal doesn't strike me as your typical rancher," Clark said.

"Ever hear of him?" Clint asked.

"Nothin'," Clark said. "What about you?"

"Only what I got from Arliss Morgan," Clint said. "The man likes to watch high-stakes poker games."

"Not play?"

Clint shook his head. "Apparently he doesn't have the nerve to play."

"Well, I guess we'll find out what kind of game he hosts," Clark said. He gave Clint a little salute and stepped out into the hall. "I'll say good night again."

Clint watched as Clark walked to the front stairway and descended, then Clint closed the door.

THIRTY-SEVEN

The next morning they were all at the table for breakfast, which was anything they wanted. The table ended up covered with steak and eggs and bacon and flapjacks, and everyone took what he felt like taking. Clint tried a little of it all, and noticed that Arliss Morgan stuck to steak and eggs, as did Arne Blom. Must be what bankers eat, he thought.

He found the food more than edible, and the coffee was good and strong, but was obviously easier to take for Morgan than the trail coffee Clint had prepared.

"Gentlemen," Deal said, standing as the breakfast plates were being cleared by two black men wearing white gloves. "You have the day to yourselves, but tonight we begin play at ten p.m. sharp. Hopefully, all of the other players will be in place then."

"What about the moneyman from Sacramento?" Dick Clark asked.

"He arrived earlier this morning, while we were having breakfast. He is in his room."

"Why not eat with us?" Arne Blom asked.

"A tray was taken to his room," Deal said. "You will all meet him tonight when he gives you your stake."

All the men stood, preparing to leave the table.

"If anyone gets hungry, just tell Mrs. Pyatt and she will have something prepared for you. If not, dinner will be served at six sharp. Please be there. I'm sure we'll all be here and assembled by then."

As they all walked away from the table, Clint noticed the Frenchman, Marceau, move up alongside Dick Clark and start talking to him. Maybe he wasn't such a phony after all and he actually did admire Clark. If that was true, it would be easy for Clint to understand.

As Clark left the dining room, Marceau was right alongside, and Clint had the feeling that Dick Clark had a new friend whether he wanted one or not.

Suddenly, Arliss Morgan was next to Clint.

"Can you beat Clark?"

"I don't know," Clint said. "He's one of the best in the country, maybe the world."

"That's not what I want to hear," Morgan said nervously. "Can you beat the Frenchman?"

"Oh, yes," Clint said.

"Just like that? You're sure you can beat him but not Clark?"

"Anybody can beat anybody if the cards fall right, Arliss," Clint said. "We'll just have to wait and see."

"Aren't you the least bit nervous about playing for all that money?" the banker asked.

"No," Clint lied.

As the banker moved away to engage their host, Clint knew that he was, indeed, nervous, even though he wasn't playing with his own money. Oh, he was in for a piece of the action, but if he lost, Arliss Morgan would be out a hundred thousand dollars. Playing for that much money, no matter who it belonged to, made a man nervous.

Unless it was a man like Dick Clark. For him this was just business as usual. It wasn't even about the money. He made plenty of money from his gambling halls and saloons. For him it was all about the action—and finding the edge.

Clint decided maybe it wasn't going to be the Frenchman sticking to Clark all day, but the other way around. By the time they started playing, Clark might be deep inside the Frenchman's head.

Calhoun had managed to keep Dave Coffin out of trouble the night before. He did that by paying two saloon girls to take Coffin back to his room and fuck his brains out until he fell asleep.

"What do we do then?" one of them asked.

"Why, darlin'," Calhoun said, "then you come to my room."

So Calhoun woke lying between a comely brunette and a chubby blonde. It was a hell of a long way from the way he used to wake up in prison.

He looked over at the blonde, who was lying on her belly, her chunky butt hiked up just slightly—but enough to make him hard.

He got behind her, straddled her and reached between her thighs to finger her pussy. She groaned, grew wet even before she woke up. That happened when he slid his hard dick up and into her. She gasped, came awake and quickly got to her hands and knees. As he drove himself into her, she pushed back against him. The sound of slapping flesh—not to mention the moaning and groaning—woke the other girl, who propped herself up on an elbow and watched while she touched herself.

The blonde had so much golden pubic hair that Calhoun could feel it close in around him when he slid all the way into her. It excited him even more. He'd missed pussy when he was inside, missed it badly, and he loved when there was a lot of hair around it.

The brunette herself had quite a black thatch of hair

between her legs, and he looked over as she delved into it with her own fingers.

"That's it, sweetie," he said, "keep it warm. I'll be over there as soon as I finish here with your girlfriend."

"Don't worry, lover," she said, "I'll be ready."

He could smell that she was already wet and ready for him, so he began to fuck the blonde harder and faster.

"Don't spend yourself, lover," the brunette said. "That bitch can keep you goin' all day."

"Don't worry," he gasped, as he felt his release building up in his legs, "I've got plenty for both of you."

He exploded into the blonde with a loud groan, then pulled himself free of her and moved to the brunette, who rolled over onto her back.

"Jesus," she gasped, as he drove his hard dick into her.

The blonde was trying to catch her breath, but her eyes widened as he started to fuck the brunette, and she asked, "Wow, where've you been, handsome, in prison?"

THIRTY-EIGHT

Since the entire house was open to them, Clint decided to simply have a seat on the porch and await the arrival of the other players. This way he'd find out right off who they were.

They began to arrive shortly after breakfast. John Deal had actually come out onto the porch to sit with Clint. He asked a lot of questions and gave away nothing during a short conversation, and then two men on horseback rode up. Clint wondered if that was another banker with a proxy player.

Deal stood up and said, "Time to greet my guests."

"Mind if I join you?"

"Not at all."

They both moved to the edge of the stairs as the men rode up.

"Do you know them?"

"Actually, Mr. Adams," Deal said, "I don't know any of you. This weekend will be the first time I meet you all."

"Nice of you to open your home to strangers, Mr. Deal."

"I'm a rich man, Mr. Adams," Deal said. "I can afford to do whatever I want, whenever I want, with whomever I want. Right now I want to watch some high-stakes poker."

The two men reined in their horses and dismounted. Neither was dressed like a banker. Only one was dressed like a gambler. As they started up the steps, Clint thought he knew who they were.

"Which one of you is Mr. Deal?" the man in the black gambler's suit asked.

"I am," Deal said. "Welcome to my home. You are . . ."

"I'm Red Conrad," the man said. "This is my brother, Johnny."

"I'm pleased to meet you, Mr. Conrad," Deal said. "This is—"

"Clint Adams," Red said. "I recognize you. I saw you once in Abilene." Red put out his hand and Clint shook it. "Are you here as security?"

"No," Clint said, "I'm playing."

"Really?" Red said. "That's interesting."

Clint had been right. Red and Johnny Conrad never went anywhere without each other. Johnny was basically Red's security against being attacked or robbed. Johnny was supposed to be very good with a gun—almost as good as his brother was with cards.

"This is my brother, Johnny," Red said to Clint. The two men nodded at each other. Johnny looked to be in his late twenties, while his brother looked mid-thirties.

"Mr. Conrad," Deal said, "we are asking players to give up their guns."

"It don't seem to me that Mr. Adams, here, has given up his gun."

"As I said," Deal replied, "we're asking."

"Well," Red said, "I don't carry a gun." He held his jacket open so they could see he was telling the truth. "My brother does that for both of us. But I'm afraid he won't give his up. Not with Adams armed." He looked at Clint. "No offense."

"None taken."

"If my brother has to give up his gun, I'm not playin'," Red said.

"You understand that your deposit is nonrefundable?" Deal asked.

"I do understand that," Red said. "But if Johnny can't wear his gun, we ain't even goin' in the house." He looked at Clint. "You understand."

"Perfectly."

"All right, then," Deal said. "Your brother may hold onto his gun. Come with me and I will get you situated."

Red nodded to Clint, and then he and Johnny followed Deal up the stairs. As they went into the house, Clint heard Red say, "My brother and me will need to be in the same room."

Clint was still on the porch when the next player rode up to the house alone. The horses the Conrads had ridden in on had been taken to the livery, and John Deal was still somewhere inside the house. Clint decided to walk down the stairs and greet the man.

As he reached the bottom step, the man dismounted. He was tall and had obviously ridden a long way. He turned and locked eyes with Clint.

"You Deal?" he asked.

"No," Clint said, "he's inside. I'm Clint Adams."

The man's eyes narrowed. "They got the Gunsmith for security?"

"No," Clint said, "I'm playing."

"So am I," the man said. He extended his and. "Micah McCall."

Clint didn't know the name. He shook hands with the man, who didn't look like he could afford to put up a hundred thousand dollars for a poker game. Everything he was wearing had age to it—not old and worn out, just . . . well-worn. Even the horse.

"Somebody take care of my horse?" he asked.

"Yep, somebody will take it. Come inside and I'll introduce you to our host."

McCall tied off the horse and followed Clint up the stairs.

"Is everybody here?" he asked.

"I think we're waiting for one more payer," Clint said. "He's got till ten p.m. to get here."

"Then what?"

"Then his hundred grand goes into the kitty."

"More for us."

"That's the general feeling."

Clint opened the front door, and as he did, John Deal appeared in the entryway after coming down from upstairs with Mrs. Pyatt behind him.

"Ah, another guest?" he asked.

Clint made the introductions, and Deal instructed Mrs. Pyatt to take Micah McCall to his room. McCall exchanged a nod with Clint and followed the woman up the stairs.

"You'll need to have someone take care of his horse," Clint told Deal.

"I will tend to it. Is he a proxy player?" Deal asked. "And for whom?"

"I don't think so," Clint said. "He just said he's a player."

"Micah McCall," Deal said. "Yes, I was expecting him."

"And the sixth and last player?"

"Will be arriving this afternoon."

"Why can't we get started as soon as they arrive?"

"I appreciate your eagerness to start playing, Mr. Adams, but we will have dinner and then everyone will be able to repair to his room to get ready. At nine all the players will come downstairs and collect their stakes from my banker. At ten sharp, the game will begin. It's all settled."

"Okay," Clint said, "it's your show. You call the shots."

"Indeed," John Deal said.

THIRTY-NINE

Late in the afternoon five men rode into Gardner, led by Tom Kent. Calhoun and Coffin were waiting—one patiently and one impatiently—on wooden chairs in front of their hotel.

"About time," Coffin said.

"Dave, this is Tom Kent," Calhoun said. "Tom, my partner, Dave Coffin."

Kent and Coffin exchanged nods.

"Those are the boys I hired to help out. You boys have to share two rooms in this hotel. Split up any way you want. Tom, we got you your own room."

Kent took this as a sign of respect from the two men.

"Why don't you boys give your horses to one man? He can take them to the livery, and then you can all check in."

They all dismounted except one man, who collected the reins of the horses.

"When are we doin' this?" Kent asked as the others went inside.

"Let's get a meal into their bellies and tell them what it's all about," Calhoun said.

"Without mentioning how much money is actually at stake," Coffin added.

"Right," Calhoun said.

"And then what?"

"They're gonna play through the night," Calhoun said. "We rode out there and checked on security. They've got men patrolling the grounds, but it's a big ranch. We can slip through in the middle of the night and then take them."

"The first night?" Kent asked.

"Why not?"

"If we wait, they'll be exhausted," Kent said.

"Wait?" Coffin said. "We been waitin'—"

"Easy, Dave," Calhoun said. "Why don't you go and see that the boys get their rooms, huh?"

Coffin opened his mouth to reply, but then thought better of it and went inside.

"I thought I was your partner," Kent said.

"We're partners on this job," Calhoun said. "Dave and I were partners before I went to prison. Look, Tom, I want to do this tonight and get it over with."

"We don't know how many players there are, or who they are," Kent reminded him.

"I'm gonna say worst case we're gonna have ten or twelve men—six playing at the table. The others will be backers and the host. Now, in high-stakes games like this, the players usually give up their guns so there are no . . . accidents."

"Clint Adams is playin'," Kent said. "He ain't gonna give up his gun."

"It don't matter," Calhoun said. "We'll take him first. The rest will fall in line after that."

"You hope," Kent said. "I don't wanna have to kill all these people."

"That's why it's actually gonna work to our advantage that Adams is there," Calhoun said. "Once we get rid of him, nobody will stand up to us."

"I hope you're right."

"Go get settled in your room, Tom," Calhoun said.

"Come back down in half an hour and we'll go and eat. Then, when it gets good and dark, we'll take a ride out to the ranch."

"Okay," Kent said.

"Hey!"

'What?"

"I see you got rid of the badge."

Kent looked down at his chest.

"How do you know it ain't in my pocket?"

"You're walkin' lighter."

Kent passed Coffin as he went in, and they exchanged a nod.

"Is he gonna be a problem?" Coffin asked Calhoun.

"Maybe."

"What should we do about it?" Coffin asked.

"Well," Calhoun said, rubbing his jaw, "we really don't need him."

"But if he don't show up back in Virginia City, folks are gonna wonder."

"Yeah, they'll wonder where he is, what happened to him," Calhoun said, "but they'll never connect him to this."

"So whataya wanna do?"

"Let's all eat," Calhoun said, "see how things go, and then I'll make up my mind."

"I'll do 'im," Coffin said. "No problem."

"Like I said," Calhoun said, "we got time. Let's just see what happens."

FORTY

By the time dinner came around, the sixth player had still not arrived. Clint was once again seated to John Deal's left, with Arliss Morgan right across from him.

"There are still three hours to go before you all collect your stake from my banker, Mr. Green."

Deal inclined his head toward the other end of the table, where Mr. Green, his Sacramento banker, was sitting. He had been introduced, acknowledged as the moneyman, but no one was talking to him. Clint noticed the man was a very fussy eater and spent most of his time with his head hovering over his plate, removing or moving something.

"Well, I hope he makes it," Clint said. "I'd like to see a full table."

"You wouldn't rather have that sixth stake end up in the kitty?" Deal asked.

"Where's the sport in that?" Clint asked.

"Mr. Adams," Deal said, "you surprise me more and more."

"In a good way?"

"In a very good way."

They had dessert and then moved to the den for cigars and brandy. This time Clint took the brandy but not the cigar.

He noticed Dick Clark did the same, and was nursing the brandy.

At one point John Deal was called from the room. Clint was standing in a corner, studying some of the books on the shelves—he noticed Deal had a large selection of Mark Twain and Dickens—and noticed that the Sacramento banker was in another corner of the room, also standing alone. The Frenchman, Marceau, was still dogging Dick Clark, who looked at Clint with pleading eyes. Clint just smiled, shrugged and toasted the man with his glass.

The Conrad brothers, Red and Johnny, were talking with Micah McCall, who tonight looked every inch the gambler who could afford a hundred-thousand-dollar buy in. A diamond sparkled from each pinky and from a stick-pin in his tie.

The other two bankers, Arne Blom and Arliss Morgan, stood close together and were talking earnestly.

Deal reappeared and beckoned to Green, who set his brandy glass down and left the room to join Deal in the hallway. The two men put their heads together, had a short conversation, and then Green left and Deal entered the room.

"Gentlemen, the last player has arrived," he announced. "Allow me to introduce Mrs. Charlotte Thurmond."

"A woman?" Arne Blom said.

A woman entered the room, wearing a silk gown of greens and golds, her auburn hair piled atop her head. She had a slim waist and a full, firm bust. She appeared to be in her late thirties, but Clint knew for a fact she was at least ten years older than that. That was about how long it had been since she disappeared from Fort Griffin, Texas, after establishing herself as a female gambler who was a force to be reckoned with. At that time she had been in her late thirties, but looked ten years younger then, too. He had met her, known her slightly, never been intimate with her. He wondered if she'd recognize him on sight as a man who had known her as the notorious Lottie Deno.

Clint looked across the room at Dick Clark, wondering if he had recognized her as well.

If Charlotte Thurmond had heard what the Swedish banker Arne Blom had said—or the tone with which he'd said it—she did not reveal it. Deal took her around the room to introduce her to each man individually. Obviously, he had known all along that the final player was a woman.

When they came to Clint, Deal was about to make the introduction when Charlotte put out her hand and said, "Mr. Adams and I are acquainted."

"Indeed?" Deal asked.

"I had a different name then."

Clint kept quiet. If she wanted to mention that she had once been "Lottie Deno" it was up to her.

"Yes," she said, "I wasn't married then."

"I see."

"It's nice to see you again, Clint," she said.

"The pleasure is mine, Lottie."

Even in her late forties she was a beauty. Clint didn't have to wonder what had brought her out into the open again. It was the size of the game.

They moved on and she greeted Dick Clark with more warmth, as they had, indeed, known each other, better than she and Clint did.

"You know her?"

He turned and saw Arliss Morgan standing there.

"I knew her years ago, when she was not married and was gambling regularly."

"Is she any good?"

"She was always an excellent poker player," Clint said. "I don't know what she's been doing since then. She might be rusty."

"Let's hope so."

"Actually," Clint said, "I'd like everybody to be at the top of their game. Makes winning even better."

"And more nerve-wracking."

"Gentlemen," John Deal said, when the introductions were over, "if you will accompany me and the lady, it's time to pick up your stakes."

FORTY-ONE

John Deal led all the players—and their backers—to a room on the third floor where none of them had ever been. It was down the hall from Clint's room, but the door had always been closed. As they entered, they were all very impressed. There was a round table with a green felt top, six comfortable wooden chairs, a bar set up in one corner, and behind the bar stood Mrs. Pyatt.

"Mrs. Pyatt," John Deal said, "is an excellent bartender."

Clint was more and more impressed by the woman, but still wondered what that warning was about.

In another corner Mr. Green sat behind a desk, and on the desk he had a large, black metal box. Clint assumed that the cash for everyone's stake was inside.

"If you'll all take a place at the table, Mr. Green will bring you your stake."

The only things on the table at the moment were several sealed decks of cards. There were only six seats, so Clint assumed there would be no house dealer.

They each selected a chair and sat down. Clint ended up sitting with Red Conrad on one side and Micah McCall on the other. Directly across from him was Charlotte Thurmond.

"Mr. Green?" Deal said.

Green stood up and approached the table with the black box. One by one he placed each player's hundred-thousand-dollar stake in front of the player.

"Thank you, Mr. Green," Deal said. The banker bowed, then left the room with the black box. It occurred to Clint only then that he'd never heard Mr. Green speak.

John Deal stood by the table and said, "This is the first poker game I have ever hosted. I have seen to every detail."

"Except one," Micah McCall said. "There's no dealer."

"I assumed you would be playing dealer's choice," the Englishman said. "Was I wrong?"

"Dealer's choice is fine with me, gentlemen," Charlotte said. "Anyone object?"

No one did.

"Good," Deal said. "Then that's settled."

"Except for one thing," Red Conrad said.

"And what is that?" Deal asked.

"Who deals first?"

"First ace," Clint said.

"All right," Marceau said. "But who deals ze cards for the first ace?"

"This is silly," Clint said. "Let's just open a deck and do it."

He reached for a deck. But before he could reach one, Micah McCall grabbed his wrist.

"Why you?" he asked.

"Somebody has to do it," Clint said, "or we'll never get the game started."

"Oh, dear," Deal said, "I suppose I should have secured the services of a dealer."

"I have a suggestion," Johnny Conrad said from the corner.

"What's that, John?" his brother Red asked.

"Let the lady do it."

McCall released Clint's wrist, and Clint withdrew his arm.

"Anyone object to Mrs. Thurmond doing it?" Clint asked.

They all looked around at each other and no one objected.

"Very well," Charlotte said. She picked up a deck, opened it, shuffled it expertly and fast, and then dealt the cards out until the first ace fell in front of someone.

"Mr. Adams deals," she said.

Tom Kent was getting himself ready for the ride out to the ranch. It was finally going to happen. Six hundred thousand dollars and Diane Morgan were all going to be his.

He checked his gun, made sure it was fully loaded, then holstered it. When the knock came at his door, he answered it, gun still in the holster.

"Tito," he said, "are we ready?"

"I am," Tito Calhoun said. "You're not."

"Wha—"

Calhoun produced a small, two-shot derringer. He pushed the barrel against Kent's belly and pulled the trigger. The first shot shocked Kent and he didn't feel much pain. The second shot made his belly feel as if it was on fire.

He grabbed his stomach and staggered back into the room. Calhoun followed him in, closing the door behind him. The two quiet pops of the derringer had gone unnoticed in the hotel, just as he'd planned.

Kent's legs went out from under him, and still clutching his belly, he fell facedown on the floor, then rolled over and stared up at Calhoun.

"Why?" he asked.

"For money," Calhoun said, "and a beautiful woman. What else is there?"

FORTY-TWO

Clint dealt the first hand and won a small pot. He also won a glare from Micah McCall, and wondered if he was going to have trouble with the man.

"For the money we're playing for," the man complained as the deal passed to him, "we should have a dealer."

"I don't mind dealing my own games," Charlotte said. "Mixes things up."

"Five-card stud," McCall said, and dealt the hand out.

With Kent gone—lying dead on the floor of his hotel room in Gardner, a town Calhoun would never return to—they had six men: Calhoun, Coffin and the four men who had come to town with Kent. Those four men were not at all curious about where Kent was. They still looked at him as a lawman, and as far as they were concerned, it was good riddance.

The six men rode out to the Double-D Ranch and, in the dark, were able to slip through the sparse security patrols John Deal had arranged.

"He's bound to have better security than this at the house, though," Calhoun said to Coffin.

They were riding together, ahead of the other four men.

"That'll be for you and me to handle," Coffin said. "We can let those four take care of whatever foot patrol they have outside the house, then we slip in and take care of the inside."

"We'll have to let them in," Calhoun said. "We don't know how many guns are gonna actually be in the room with the cardplayers, but we have to take care of Clint Adams first."

They knew they would have to search the house for the room where the game was being played, unless they could get somebody to tell them.

"That shouldn't be too hard," Coffin said. "If we kill one man in front of another, then that one should talk."

"Sounds like a good plan," Calhoun said.

"You were tellin' that sheriff we were gonna wear masks," Coffin said. "What was that about?"

"I didn't want him backin' out until I was ready to get rid of him," Calhoun said.

"So no masks?"

"No masks."

"That means we're gonna do some killin'," Coffin said.

"We're gonna do some killin'."

"How much?"

Calhoun looked at his partner and said, "Everybody in or around that house."

Not to mention, they both thought, the four men riding behind them. Calhoun and Coffin were determined to be the only men walking away when it was all over.

FORTY-THREE

The first hour was a feeling-out period. The only man Clint ever played against before was Dick Clark. He had never played against Charlotte when she was Lottie Deno. He didn't know if Dick Clark had.

The Frenchman was just plain bad. He had a habit of clearing his throat when he had a good hand. Clint didn't know why the Swedish banker had chosen this man to represent his hundred thousand.

Red Conrad played his cards close to the vest in a very tight game. Clint knew that when the man raised, he had something.

Micah McCall was aggressive, which made him hard to read. He pretty much bet the same way whether he had something or not.

Dick Clark was, of course, a brilliant poker player.

Clint didn't know what Charlotte had been doing since her days as Lottie Deno, but it didn't seem to have affected her play.

After the first hour Clint was slightly ahead. He had raised on three hands and had taken them all down. He had made folds on good hands twice, once to Dick Clark's full house and once to Charlotte's flush. Five good hands out of six played the first time around the table, and he had won three of them.

"You're a lucky man," Micah McCall said to Clint as they started the second time around the table.

"Luck's got nothing to do with it," Clint said. "It's all skill." He wanted to get under the man's skin.

He thought he was succeeding.

Dave Coffin snuck behind one of the guards. One arm snaked around the man's neck, and before he could make a sound, a knife was thrust into his back. The man bucked and shuddered. Coffin lowered him to the ground gently and released him when he knew he was dead.

On the other side of the house Calhoun had his arm around the neck of a guard. He and Coffin had agreed that they should probably be the ones to take out the guards. The other four men were just guns at the end of an arm. They were for show. They didn't want to have to depend on them for anything fancy.

He tightened his arm and asked in the man's ear, "How many guards inside?"

"Two."

"Where?"

"Downstairs."

"What floor is the game being played on?"

"We don't know," the guard said. "They didn't tell—"

Calhoun snapped the man's neck and lowered the body to the ground, then he waved for the four other men to join him. They were all hiding near the barn, and came running at the same moment Coffin came around from the side of the house.

"See anybody else?" Calhoun asked him.

"No, just those two."

"You can tell this jasper has never hosted a high-stakes poker game before," Calhoun said. "His security is a joke."

"Good for us," Coffin said.

'Very good for us," Calhoun said. "According to this one there are two guards inside the house, both on the first floor."

"Let's go, then." Coffin turned to the other men. "No shootin' unless we say, got it?"

"We got it," one of them said.

Coffin didn't know his name, but it didn't matter. As far as he was concerned, they were faceless and nameless. And soon to be dead.

FORTY-FOUR

During the second hour everyone was deeply into the game, especially the spectators.

Arliss Morgan was very nervous, even though Clint was doing well. He leaned forward on every hand, holding his breath until the last card was dealt and the last bet was made. Arne Blom had quickly decided his man was overmatched and could only rely on luck. The Frenchman himself remained arrogant, but he was either posturing or clueless.

Conrad and McCall were losing. Conrad seemed unconcerned; McCall was growing more agitated. Clint knew Conrad had given up his gun. He assumed McCall had, too, since he saw no telltale bulge—unless the man had an expert tailor.

As far as Clint knew or could tell, he and Johnny Conrad were the only ones in the room who were armed.

Unless Mrs. Pyatt, still standing behind the bar, had a gun.

Downstairs, Calhoun, Coffin and their men had rounded up every member of the staff and gathered them in the kitchen. On the floor were the two guards, both dead.

"What the hell do they need all these people for?" Coffin

asked, looking around the kitchen at the men and women who worked for John Deal.

"Cooking, cleaning," Calhoun said, "whatever else a rich man wants done." He thought that once he got away from here with his money, maybe he'd have a house like this, with people working for him.

Coffin pointed to one of the dead guards.

"He said the game's on the third floor. That's the top."

"What do we do with all these people?" one of Calhoun's men asked.

"Tie 'em up for now," Calhoun said. "We don't want to risk them makin' any noise." He turned to Coffin, and they both turned their backs as he said, "We can finish them later."

Coffin nodded and turned back.

" 'Course, any of you wanna scream, we'll just shoot the bunch of you and deal with it."

"Ain't nobody goin' ta scream," one of the black hostages said.

"Lookit this," Coffin said. "Four women and two black men. Don't you fellas know you was freed by the war?"

"We's freemen, suh," one of them said. "We gets paid."

"Not enough, I'll bet," Calhoun said.

"No, suh," the other one said, "not hardly enuff."

While Clint was sitting out a hand, he noticed Mrs. Pyatt call John Deal over to the bar. They put their heads together and she spoke urgently. He nodded and moved away. Clint stood up and walked over to the man.

"What's wrong?"

"Somebody was supposed to have brought up sandwiches a while ago," he said. "Mrs. Pyatt wanted to go find out why they haven't done so, but I told her to stay put, I'd go."

"Is your staff usually prompt?"

"Very. This is unusual. Somebody's going to get fired. One or the other of my security men was also to have checked in with me every hour. We're into hour two, and I haven't seen any of them. Yes, someone is going to get fired."

He started to turn away, but Clint grabbed his arm.

"Tell me your security setup."

Deal outlined it briefly, inside and out, and Clint realized how woefully inadequate it was. He should have asked before.

"Stay here," he said. "I'll go and check."

"You think something may be wrong?" Deal asked.

"You tell me," Clint said. "Your house staff and security have failed to do their job. Why would that be?"

"Oh, dear," John Deal said. "I had assumed they were simply inept."

"Well," Clint said, "that could be. It could also be that they're all dead."

"But . . . this is a private game." Deal sounded puzzled. "I kept it all very hush-hush."

"How many people work in the house?"

"Seven."

"That, and the security men you brought in—somebody had to have talked." Clint was thinking about Arliss Morgan's young wife.

"How many guns are in this room?" Clint asked.

"Just you and Mr. Conrad, the younger."

"That's what I thought. Stay in this room, and keep everyone else in."

Clint waved his hand at Johnny, got his attention and called him over.

"You and me are going to check the house."

"Somethin' wrong?"

"Maybe. We're the only ones with guns."

Johnny turned to look at his brother, who was concentrating on his cards.

"Let's go," Johnny said.

As he opened the door, Clint heard Micah McCall ask, "Now where's he goin'? . . ."

FORTY-FIVE

Clint and Johnny Conrad slipped out of the room and into the hall, moving as silently as possible. Clint signaled for Johnny to go to the back stairs while Clint would check the front. Johnny nodded. They separated, both with their guns in hand. Clint watched as Johnny reached the end of the hall and started down.

There was no way to see down to the first floor, and even from the top of the stairs Clint would not be able to see much of the second. He cursed inwardly. He should have told Johnny not to go down, just to wait. If there was somebody in the house with the intention of taking down the game, they'd have to come up. All Clint and Johnny had to do was wait. Of course, there were the lives of the staff and the guards to consider. By going down, they might end up saving lives.

And, of course, there was always the possibility John Deal's staff actually *was* inept.

Clint decided to chance it and go down the stairs to the second floor. No one could get past him, and if Johnny got into trouble, he'd be able to hear it. As quickly as the younger man had been moving, he was probably already down one level.

Clint started moving toward the head of the stairs . . .

* * *

Calhoun, Coffin and the other four had made it as far as the second floor. They could see the stairs leading up to the third. They did not see, nor did they know, that there was another staircase in the back.

"There might be anther stairway in a house this size," Calhoun said.

"What does that matter?" Coffin asked. "Here's the stairs. The directions we got to the room are from this staircase. Let's just go up and do this."

"Okay," Calhoun said. "You four go up first. When you get to the top, wait."

None of the four men cared who went up first. The staircase was wide enough for them to go two or three abreast, so they went three with the fourth man behind them. Calhoun and Coffin brought up the rear, coming side by side.

None of them had their guns out.

Johnny Conrad made it to the second floor quickly and without incident. He hadn't taken the time to think about it that Clint had. He'd gone straight down, and now he had a decision. Keep going down to the first, or check out the rest of the second? He decided to go down to the first, and he did so as fast and quietly as he could. When he got there, he discovered he was in the kitchen. And when he saw the assemblage of people lying on the floor, good and hogtied, he turned and ran back up, yelling, "Somebody's in the house! Adams!"

Clint was being infinitely more deliberate than Johnny Conrad was. He was moving slowly, making his way to the head of the stairs. As he reached there and started down, he saw three men abreast starting up. He stopped short. They hadn't seen him yet, but all they had to do was look up. He had started to back up when he heard Johnny shouting something. He couldn't make it out, but the other men heard it as well. They looked up, and froze.

Calhoun heard the shouting and knew, somehow, the people in the kitchen had been discovered.

"Go, go, go!" he shouted to the men ahead of him. He had not yet seen Clint Adams.

Clint had no choice. He drew and fired in one swift motion. The three-man plateau below him all went for guns, but they were slow, and they were getting in one another's way. It took three shots from Clint's gun to stop them all.

As the three men came tumbling back down the stairs, they knocked the fourth man down. Coffin leaped back, avoiding the spill, and Calhoun was behind him.

"Damn it!" Calhoun said. "There's got to be another stairway. Hold him!" he shouted.

Coffin turned, but Calhoun was already running to the other end of the floor. Coffin grabbed the fourth man and pulled him to his feet, firing blindly up the stairs as he did.

Calhoun was only thinking about the money on the floor above him. He reached the back stairway and saw a man running up ahead of him. He had no qualms about shooting a man in the back, and that's what he did.

Johnny Conrad had no idea what had happened to him. He'd never been shot before. Something slammed into his back and then he was falling, tumbling back down the stairs, his gun flying from his hand . . .

Clint ducked the shots coming from the bottom of the stairs. The shot from the back stairs had blended in. He didn't know how many more men were there, but his best

play now was to stay on the third floor and let them come
to him.

Suddenly, it got quiet, and a voice called from downstairs.

"Adams? Is that you? Clint Adams? You ain't got a
chance. We got a dozen men in the house."

Clint knew that was a lie, but he still didn't know how
many men there were.

"Come on down, Adams," the voice said. "Come on
down and we'll talk. We'll cut you in."

Clint froze at the top of the stairs, waiting.

Calhoun reached the third floor and slowed himself down.
He didn't want to run headlong into anything. He stuck his
head around so he could look down the hall, saw a man
standing at the top of the stairs and assumed it had to be
Clint Adams. If he'd been looking for a reputation, he
would have shot the man, but Adams was staring down and
Calhoun could hear Coffin talking to him. Firing a shot
would alert the man to his presence. If he moved quickly
and quietly enough, he could get to the room with the
money.

He stepped into the hall and started down it as fast as he
could without attracting Clint Adams's attention.

Inside the room all the players and spectators had frozen
and were now simply listening for the shots.

"Somebody go out there and help them!" Charlotte
Thurmond shouted.

"Mrs. Thurmond," Micah McCall said, "thanks to Mr.
Deal, we have no guns. We'd just get in the way."

Charlotte glared at Dick Clark.

"Well," he said, standing, "I guess we should try to do
something."

He caught some movement from the corner of his eyes
and saw Mrs. Pyatt waving to him from the bar.

* * *

Clint decided to try something else. If he could get to the back stairs and down to the second floor, he could come up behind the gunmen—however many of them were left.

As he turned to move up the hallway, he saw a man in front of the door to the game. He had a gun in one hand and the doorknob in another.

"Hold it!"

If that man got inside the room, he'd have a host of hostages.

Clint brought his gun around to fire, and as he did two men appeared at the bottom of the stairs . . .

Coffin heard Clint Adams shout, figured Calhoun had gotten around behind him.

"Take him! Take him!" he shouted to the one man he had left.

They both mounted the stairs and aimed their guns at Clint.

Again, Clint had no choice. If he fired at the man in the hall, the two on the stairs would kill him.

"Damn it!"

He turned his gun to the stairs and he and the two men there all fired at the same time, only the men fired once each and Clint fired twice. He felt something lick at his left arm, but he stood fast and put a bullet into each man's chest, then ran down the hall.

Calhoun entered the room without a shot from Clint Adams. The first thing he saw was the green felt table filled with chips. He looked around, didn't see a gun pointed at him.

"Where's the money?" he demanded.

"My good man—" Deal started.

Calhoun turned on him and decided to make him the example for the rest. Before he could fire, there was a shot and something stung him in the side of the neck. The strength went out of his arm and he groped for his gun as his mouth filled with blood.

At that moment Clint rushed in, just in time to see Calhoun fall.

FORTY-SIX

They sent for a lawman from Gardner. In a conversation with Clint, the sheriff mentioned that they'd had a murder in town, a man named Tom Kent.

"Kent?" Clint asked.

"That's right. You know him?" Sheriff Jeff Owen asked.

"Well, yes, he's the sheriff of Virginia City."

Sheriff Owen assumed that Kent had followed the gang to Gardner, tried to stop them from robbing the game, and was killed for his trouble. Clint thought there could have been another possibility—that Kent was in on it with them—but decided to keep his mouth shut.

The sheriff and some of his men loaded the bodies onto a buckboard and took them to town for the undertaker.

Clint joined John Deal on the front steps as the sheriff and his men pulled away.

"It was my fault," Deal said.

"How so?"

"My security measures were . . . inadequate."

"Well, yes," Clint said.

"If not for you, we'd all be dead," Deal said. "Not just my guards." Deal turned to Clint. "You saved me, my staff and everybody in that room."

"Johnny Conrad had something to do with that," Clint said.

"Yes, he did. His brother is taking his body home, so he won't be playing tonight."

"The game is going to go on?" Clint asked.

"Well, yes," Deal said. "There is a lot of money involved."

"That's what those men thought," Clint said. "They didn't know that the money was in a bank in Sacramento and that the only thing on the table in that room were chips."

"The winner will have to go to Sacramento, to Mr. Green's bank, to collect the money."

"So all those men were killed for nothing," Clint said.

"Yes," Deal said.

"You're right, Mr. Deal," Clint said.

"About what?"

"It was your fault."

Clint went down the steps and headed for the livery to saddle Eclipse. He didn't want anything further to do with this game.

"Clint!"

He turned when he heard his name, and saw Arliss Morgan trotting toward him.

"You're not leaving," the banker said.

"I am."

"But what about the game?"

"You'll have to play for yourself," Clint said. "A lot of men were killed last night. I can't just forget that and sit down to play poker."

"But—"

"No buts, Arliss," Clint said. "And if I were you, I'd check with your wife when you get back to Virginia City."

"My wife?"

"She's the only one you gave all the details to, right?"

"She wouldn't—"

"Don't kid yourself," Clint said. "Most women would for that much money."

"Look, I'll make your end bigger—"

"It's not the money, Arliss," Clint said. "I don't need the money."

"Well, I do," the man hissed. "I need to cover certain . . . reversals."

"You did steal money from your own bank, didn't you?" Morgan stood speechless.

"It's all in your hands now, Arliss," Clint said. "I'm done."

He left the banker standing there with his mouth open, then Clint headed for the barn.

He didn't know how many of the other players were staying, and it really didn't matter. He wouldn't think any less of them. There was a lot of money involved, as Morgan and Deal both said. And for men who gambled for a living—like Dick Clark and Micah McCall—it was all about the money.

It just wasn't about the money for him.

Watch for

THE VALLEY OF THE WENDIGO

317th novel in the exciting GUNSMITH series
from Jove

Coming in May!

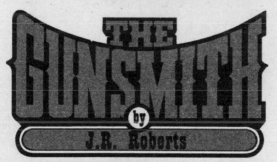